CHARLES DICKENS

OLIVER TWIST

Edited and abridged by
Latif Doss

Longman

LONGMAN GROUP UK LIMITED
Longman House, Burnt Mill, Harlow,
Essex CM20 2JE, England
and Associated Companies throughout the world.

© Longman Group Ltd 1962

First published in this edition 1962
Seventy-second impression 1991

ISBN 0-582-53014-8

Produced by Longman Group (FE) Ltd
Printed in Hong Kong

THE BRIDGE SERIES

The *Bridge Series* is intended for students of English as a second or foreign language who have progressed beyond the elementary graded readers and the *Longman Simplified English Series* but are not yet sufficiently advanced to read works of literature in their original form.

The books in the *Bridge Series* are moderately simplified in vocabulary and often slightly reduced in length, but with little change in syntax. The purpose of the texts is to give practice in understanding fairly advanced sentence patterns and to help in the appreciation of English style. We hope that they will prove enjoyable to read for their own sake and that they will at the same time help students to reach the final objective of reading original works of literature in English with full understanding and appreciation.

Technical Note
The vocabulary of the *Simplified English Series* is the 2,000 words of the *General Service List* (*Interim Report on Vocabulary Selection*) and there is a degree of structure control. In the *Bridge Series* words outside the commonest 7,000 (in Thorndike and Lorge: *A Teacher's Handbook of 30,000 Words*, Columbia University, 1944) have usually been replaced by commoner and more generally useful words. Words used which are outside the first 3,000 of the list are explained in a glossary and are so distributed throughout the book that they do not occur at a greater density than 25 per running 1,000 words.

Contents

Introduction

Charles Dickens was born near Portsmouth in 1812, one of a family of six. His parents were very poor. His father ran heavily into debt and when Charles was twelve, he had to go and work in a factory for making boot polish. These were the kind of conditions in which Charles Dickens grew up and, as a result, the only formal education he received was two years at a very poor school. In fact, he had to teach himself all he knew. He worked for a time as a junior clerk in a lawyer's office, and was then employed by a newspaper as a parliamentary reporter in the House of Commons.

It was at the age of twenty-four that Dickens began to write the novels for which he is now famous. He was a great observer of people and places and, in particular, he was attracted by life and conditions in mid-nineteenth century London. He writes at his best when he is describing the characters of people, particularly those of the lower-middle class, or those of little education. Many of his novels like *Oliver Twist*, *Nicholas Nickleby* and *David Copperfield* drew attention to the unsatisfactory social conditions that existed in England over a hundred years ago, and in a few cases they helped to have them improved.

Chapter 1

Oliver Twist is born

Oliver Twist was born in a workhouse, and for a long time after his birth there was considerable doubt whether the child would live. He lay breathless for some time, rather unequally balanced between this world and the next. After a few struggles, however, he breathed, sneezed and uttered a loud cry.

The pale face of a young woman lying on the bed was raised weakly from the pillow and in a faint voice she said, "Let me see the child and die."

"Oh, you must not talk about dying yet," said the doctor, as he rose from where he was sitting near the fire and advanced towards the bed.

"God bless her, no!" added the poor old pauper who was acting as nurse.

The doctor placed the child in its mother's arms; she pressed her cold white lips on its forehead; passed her hands over her face; gazed wildly around, fell back—and died.

"It's all over," said the doctor at last.

"Ah, poor dear, so it is!" said the old nurse.

"She was a good-looking girl, too," added the doctor; "where did she come from?"

"She was brought here last night," replied the old woman. "She was found lying in the street. She had walked some distance, for her shoes were torn to pieces; but where she came from, or where she was going, nobody knows."

"The old story," said the doctor, shaking his head, as he leaned over the body, and raised the left hand; "no wedding ring, I see. Ah! Good night!"

Chapter 2

Early years

For the next eight or ten months Oliver was brought up by hand. Then he was sent to a branch-workhouse some three miles off, where twenty or thirty other young parentless children rolled about the floor all day, without the inconvenience of too much food or too much clothing. They were under the charge of an elderly woman called Mrs Mann who received from the government sevenpence halfpenny weekly for each child. Being a woman of wisdom and experience she knew what was good for the children and what was good for herself. So she kept the greater part of the weekly money for her own use, and gave the children in her charge hardly enough to keep them alive.

It cannot be expected that this system of bringing up children would produce any very extraordinary or strong ones. Oliver Twist's ninth birthday found him a pale, weak child, very thin and rather below average height. But the child was full of spirit.

He was keeping his ninth birthday in the coal-cellar with two other children; they had, all three, been beaten by Mrs Mann and then locked up for daring to say they were hungry.

Suddenly, Mrs Mann was startled by the appearance of Mr Bumble, a workhouse official; a fat man, full of a sense of his own importance. The purpose of his visit was to take Oliver back to the workhouse, for he was now too old to remain with Mrs Mann.

Oliver, whose face and hands had by this time been washed in a hurry, was led into the room by his kind-hearted protectress.

" Make a bow to the gentleman, Oliver," said Mrs Mann.

2

Oliver obeyed.

"Will you go along with me, Oliver?" said Mr Bumble in a majestic voice.

Oliver was about to say that he would readily go along with anybody, when, looking upward, he caught sight of Mrs Mann, who had got behind Mr. Bumble's chair, and was shaking her fist at him. He understood what she meant at once.

"Will *she* go with me?" asked poor Oliver.

"No, she can't," replied Mr. Bumble. "But she'll come and see you sometimes."

Oliver pretended to be very sad at going away; it was easy for him to call tears into his eyes. Hunger and recent bad treatment are great helpers if you want to cry; and Oliver cried very naturally indeed. Mrs Mann gave him a thousand kisses, and, what Oliver wanted a great deal more, a piece of bread and butter, lest he should seem too hungry when he got to the workhouse. Oliver was led away by Mr Bumble from the miserable home where one kind word or look had never lighted the darkness of his early years.

Life in the workhouse was very severe indeed. The members of the board which managed it had made a rule that the children should work to earn their living, and that they should be given three meals of thin soup a day, with an onion twice a week and half a cake on Sundays.

The room in which the boys were fed was a large stone hall, with a huge pot at one end: out of which the master, assisted by one or two women, served out the soup at meal-times. Each boy had one small bowl, and no more—except on feast days, when he had two ounces and a quarter of bread besides. The bowls never needed washing. The boys polished them with their spoons till they shone again, and when they had performed this operation they would sit staring at the huge pot, with such eager eyes, as if they could have eaten it up.

Oliver Twist and his companions suffered the pangs of slow starvation for three months; at last they got so wild with hunger that one boy, who was tall for his age, told his companions that unless he had another bowl of soup every day, he was afraid he might some night eat the boy who slept next to him. He had a wild hungry eye, and they fully believed him. A council was held; lots were cast who should walk up to the master after supper that evening, and ask for more; and it fell to Oliver Twist.

The evening arrived; the boys took their places. The master, in his cook's uniform, stood beside the huge pot, with his two assistants behind him; the soup was served out. It quickly disappeared; the boys whispered to each other and made signs to Oliver. He rose from the table; and advancing to the master, bowl in hand, said, " Please, sir, I want some more."

The master was a fat, healthy man; but he turned very pale. He gazed with horror and astonishment on the small boy for some seconds.

" What! " he said at length in a faint voice.

" Please, sir," replied Oliver, " I want some more."

The master aimed a blow at Oliver's head with his big spoon; held him tight in his arms; and cried aloud for Mr Bumble.

Mr Bumble, hearing the cry, and learning the cause for it, rushed into the room where the board were sitting in a solemn meeting, and addressing the gentleman in the high chair, said,

" Mr Limbkins, I beg your pardon, sir. Oliver Twist has asked for more."

There was a general alarm. Horror was on every face.

" For *more*! " said Mr Limbkins. " Be calm, Bumble, and answer me clearly. Do you mean to say that he asked for more, after he had eaten the supper given by the board? "

" He did, sir," replied Bumble.

"That boy will be hanged," said one of the gentlemen on the board. "I know that boy will be hanged."

Oliver was locked up at once; and next morning a notice was put up on the outside of the gate, offering a reward of five pounds to anybody who would take Oliver Twist off the hands of the workhouse. In other words, five pounds and Oliver Twist were offered to any man or woman who wanted an apprentice to any trade or business.

Chapter 3

A chimney-sweep offers to take Oliver

For weeks after committing the crime of asking for more, Oliver remained a prisoner in the dark and lonely room to which he had been sent as punishment by the board. But let it not be supposed by the enemies of "the system" that Oliver, while a prisoner, was denied the benefit of exercise, or the pleasure of society. As for exercise, it was nice cold weather, and he was allowed to wash himself every morning under the pump, in a stone yard, in the presence of Mr Bumble, who prevented his catching cold, and caused a warm feeling to go through his body, by a repeated use of the stick. As for society, he was carried every other day into the hall where the boys dined, and there publicly beaten as a warning and example.

It chanced one morning that Mr Gamfield, a chimney-sweep, went his way down the High Street, deeply thinking of how to pay certain rents he owed to his landlord. Passing the workhouse, his eyes fell on the notice on the gate. He walked up to the gate to read it.

One of the gentlemen on the board was standing at the

gate. The chimney sweep, observing him, told him that he wanted an apprentice and was ready to take the boy offered. The gentleman ordered him to walk in and he took him to Mr Limbkins.

The bargain was made. Mr Bumble was at once instructed that Oliver Twist and papers of his apprenticeship were to be taken before the magistrate, for approval, that very afternoon.

On his way to the magistrate, Mr Bumble instructed Oliver that all he would have to do would be to look very happy, and say, when the gentleman asked him if he wanted to be apprenticed, that he should like it very much indeed.

Presently they arrived at the office and appeared before the magistrate, an old gentleman with a pair of eye-glasses.

"This is the boy, your worship," said Mr Bumble. "Bow to the magistrate, my dear."

Oliver made his best bow.

"Well," said the old gentleman. "I suppose he's fond of chimney-sweeping?"

"He's very fond of it, your worship," replied Bumble, giving Oliver a pinch.

"And he *will* be a sweep, will he?" inquired the old gentleman.

"If he was to be apprenticed to any other trade tomorrow, he'd run away, your worship," replied Bumble.

"And this man that's to be his master—you, sir—you'll treat him well, and feed him, and do all that sort of thing, will you?" said the old gentleman.

"When I say I will, I mean I will," replied Mr Gamfield roughly.

"You're a rough speaker, my friend, but you look an honest, open-hearted man," said the old gentleman, turning his eye-glasses in the direction of Gamfield, on whose face cruelty was clearly stamped. But the magistrate was half blind, so he couldn't reasonably be expected to see what other people saw.

The magistrate fixed his eye-glasses more firmly on his nose, and began to look about him for the inkpot.

It was the critical moment of Oliver's fate. If the inkpot had been where the old gentleman thought it was, he would have been led away at once. But as it chanced to be immediately under his nose, he looked all over his desk for it, without finding it; and happening in the course of his search to look straight before him, his gaze met the pale and frightened face of Oliver Twist, who was regarding the fearful face of his future master with a mixture of horror and fear.

The old gentleman stopped, laid down his pen, and looked from Oliver to Mr Bumble.

"My boy!" said the old gentleman, leaning over the desk, "you look pale and alarmed. What is the matter? Stand a little way from him, Mr Bumble. Now, boy, tell us what's the matter: don't be afraid."

Oliver fell on his knees, and joining his hands together, prayed the magistrate that he would order him back to the dark room—starve him—beat him—kill him if he liked—rather than send him away with that dreadful man.

"Well!" said Mr Bumble, raising his hands and eyes in a very solemn manner. "Well! Of all the cunning orphans that I have ever seen, you are one of the most shameless."

"Hold your tongue," said the magistrate. "I refuse to sign these papers," pushing them aside as he spoke. "Take the boy back to the workhouse, and treat him kindly. He seems to need it."

The next morning the public were once more informed that Oliver Twist was again to let, and that five pounds would be paid to anybody who would take possession of him.

Chapter 4

Oliver is apprenticed to an undertaker

Mr Bumble was returning one day to the workhouse when he met at the gate Mr Sowerberry, the undertaker, a tall, bony man dressed in a worn-out black suit. As he advanced to Mr Bumble he shook him by the hand and said:

"I have taken the measure of the two women that died last night, Mr Bumble."

"You'll make your fortune, Mr Sowerberry," said Mr Bumble.

"Think so?" said the undertaker. "The prices allowed by the board are very small, Mr Bumble."

"So are the coffins," replied the latter.

Mr Sowerberry laughed a long time at this joke. "Well, well, Mr Bumble," he said at length, "I don't deny that, since the new system of feeding has come in, the coffins are somewhat narrower and more shallow than they used to be; but we must have some profit, Mr Bumble. Wood is expensive, sir."

"Well, well," said Mr Bumble, "every trade has its disadvantages. By the way, you don't know anybody who wants a boy, do you?"

"Ah!" exclaimed the undertaker, "that's the very thing I wanted to speak to you about. You know, Mr Bumble, I think I'll take the boy myself."

Mr Bumble grasped the undertaker by the arm and led him into the building, where it was quickly arranged that Oliver should go to him that evening.

Oliver heard this news in perfect silence, and carrying a brown paper parcel in his hand, which was all the luggage he had, he was led away by Mr Bumble to a new scene of suffering.

For some time they walked on in silence. As they drew near to Mr Sowerberry's shop Mr Bumble looked down to make sure that the boy was in good order to be seen by his new master.

"Oliver!" said Mr Bumble. "Pull that cap off your eyes, and hold up your head."

Oliver did as he was told at once, but when he looked up at Mr Bumble there were tears in his eyes. Mr Bumble _____ him. The child made a strong effort _____ the tears rolled down his cheeks and _____ with both his hands.

_____ Mr Bumble, stopping short and _____ly, "of all the most ungrateful and _____ ever seen, Oliver, you are the——"

_____ Oliver, clinging to the hand which _____, sir; I will be good indeed; indeed I _____ttle boy, sir; and it is so—so——"

_____ Mr Bumble in amazement.

_____ry lonely!" cried the child.

_____aker had just closed his shop and was writing the details of the day's business by the light of the candle when Mr Bumble entered.

"Here, Mr Sowerberry, I've brought the boy."

"Oh! that's the boy, is it?" said the undertaker, raising the candle above his head, to get a better view of Oliver. "Mrs Sowerberry, will you have the goodness to come here a moment, my dear?"

Mrs Sowerberry, a short, thin, quarrelsome woman, came from a little room behind the shop.

"My dear," said Mr Sowerberry, respectfully, "this is the boy from the workhouse that I told you of."

"Dear me!" she said. "He's very small."

"Why, he is rather small," replied Mr Bumble, "but he'll grow, Mrs Sowerberry—he'll grow."

"Ah! I dare say he will," replied the lady angrily, "on

our food and drink. I see no saving in workhouse children, not I; for they always cost more to keep than they are worth. However, men always think they know best. There! Get downstairs, little bag of bones."

The undertaker's wife opened a side door and pushed Oliver down some stairs into a damp and dark room which was used as a kitchen. In it sat an untidy girl in worn-out shoes and torn blue stockings.

"Here, Charlotte," said Mrs Sowerberry, who had followed Oliver down, "give this boy some of the cold bits that were put up for the dog. He hasn't come home since the morning, so he may go without them."

Oliver's eyes shone at the mention of meat; a plateful of coarse broken pieces was set before him; and he ate greedily, Mrs Sowerberry regarding him with silent horror. When he had finished she said:

"Come with me," and, taking a dim and dirty lamp, she led the way upstairs. "Your bed is under the counter. You don't mind sleeping among the coffins, I suppose? But it doesn't matter whether you do or don't, for you can't sleep anywhere else."

Oliver obediently followed his new mistress.

Chapter 5

Noah Claypole

Oliver, being left to himself in the undertaker's shop, set the lamp down on a bench, and gazed fearfully about him. An unfinished coffin which stood in the middle of the shop looked so gloomy and death-like that a cold tremble came over him, every time his eyes wandered in its direction, and he almost expected to see some frightful form raise its head out of it, to drive him mad with terror.

He was awakened in the morning by a loud kicking at the outside of the shop door. When he began to unfasten the chain an angry voice began:

"Open the door, will you?"

"I will, directly, sir," replied Oliver, unfastening the chain and turning the key.

"I suppose you're the new boy, ain't you?" said the voice through the key-hole.

"Yes, sir," replied Oliver.

"How old are you?" inquired the voice.

"Ten, sir," replied Oliver.

"Then I'll whip you when I get in," said the voice, and having made this kind promise, the speaker began to whistle.

Oliver drew back the bolts with a trembling hand, and opened the door. He looked up the street and down the street; he saw nobody but a big charity-boy, sitting on a post in front of the house, eating a slice of bread and butter.

"I beg your pardon, sir," said Oliver at length, seeing that no other visitor made his appearance, "did you knock?"

"I kicked," replied the charity-boy.

"Did you want a coffin, sir?" inquired Oliver, innocently.

At this the charity-boy looked fierce and said that Oliver would want one before long, if he made jokes with his superiors in that way.

"You don't know who I am, I suppose, Workhouse?" said the charity-boy, descending from the top of the post.

"No, sir," replied Oliver.

"I'm Mister Noah Claypole," said the charity-boy. "And you're under me. Take down the shutters, you idle young ruffian." With this, Mr Claypole gave Oliver a kick and entered the shop.

Mr and Mrs Sowerberry came down soon after. Oliver followed Noah downstairs.

"Come near the fire, Noah," said Charlotte. "I saved a nice little bit of bacon for you from the master's breakfast. Oliver, shut that door at Mister Noah's back, and take your tea to that box and drink it there. Do you hear?"

"Do you hear, Workhouse?" said Noah Claypole.

At this Charlotte burst into a hearty laugh in which she was joined by Noah; after which they both looked scornfully at poor Oliver Twist, as he sat trembling on the box in the coldest corner of the room, and ate the broken pieces which had been specially reserved for him.

Noah was a charity-boy, but not a workhouse orphan. His mother was a washerwoman and his father a drunken soldier. For several months Oliver endured the ill-treatment of Noah without complaint, until one day something happened which indirectly produced a material change in Oliver's life.

Oliver and Noah had descended into the kitchen at the usual dinner hour. Noah put his feet on the table-cloth, pulled Oliver's hair and pinched his ear, in order to annoy him. Seeing that Oliver did not cry he said to him:

"Workhouse! How's your mother?"

"She's dead," replied Oliver; "don't you say anything about her to me!"

Oliver's colour rose as he said this; he breathed quickly; and there was a curious movement in the mouth and nostrils, which Mr Claypole thought must be signs of an approaching violent fit of crying. He therefore returned to his insulting words.

"What did she die of, Workhouse?" he said.

"Of a broken heart, some of our old nurses told me," replied Oliver, as a tear rolled down his cheek.

"What has made you cry now?"

12

"Not you," replied Oliver, hastily brushing the tear away. "Don't you think it."

"Oh, not me, eh!" said Noah.

"No, not you," replied Oliver, sharply. "There, that's enough. Don't say anything more to me about her; you'd better not!"

"Better not!" exclaimed Noah. "Well! Better not! Workhouse, don't be impudent. *Your* mother, too! She was a nice one, she was. Oh, God! You know, Workhouse, your mother was a bad woman."

"What did you say?" inquired Oliver, looking up very quickly.

"A bad woman, Workhouse," replied Noah coolly. "And it's a good thing she died when she did, or else she would have been doing hard labour in prison, or she might have been hanged, which is more likely."

Red with anger, Oliver started up, overthrew the chair and table; seized Noah by the throat; shook him till his teeth chattered in his head, and, collecting his whole force into one heavy blow, felled him to the ground.

"He'll murder me!" shouted Noah. "Charlotte! Missis! The new boy is murdering me! Help! Help! Oliver's gone mad! Char—lotte!"

Noah's shouts were answered by a loud scream from Charlotte, and a louder one from Mrs Sowerberry, and they both rushed into the kitchen.

"Oh, you little wretch!" screamed Charlotte, seizing Oliver with all her force, and giving him several blows and screaming at the same time.

Mrs Sowerberry held Oliver with one hand, and scratched his face with the other. In this favourable position of affairs Noah rose from the ground and beat him with his fist from behind. When they were all tired out, and could tear and beat no longer, they dragged Oliver, struggling and shouting, into the cellar, and there locked him up. This being done, Mrs Sowerberry sank into a chair, and burst into tears.

"Bless her, she's about to faint!" said Charlotte. "A glass of water, Noah, dear. Make haste!"

"Oh! Charlotte," said Mrs Sowerberry, almost unable to breathe from the cold water which Noah had poured over her head and shoulders. "Oh! Charlotte, what a mercy we have not all been murdered in our beds!"

"Ah! mercy indeed, ma'am," was the reply. "I only hope this will teach master not to have any more of these dreadful creatures, that are born to be murderers and robbers. Poor Noah! He was all but killed, ma'am, when I came in."

"Poor fellow!" said Mrs Sowerberry, looking piteously at the charity-boy. "What's to be done! Your master's not at home; there's not a man in the house, and he'll kick that door down in ten minutes."

"Dear, dear. I don't know, ma'am," said Charlotte, "unless we send for the police-officers."

"No, no," said Mrs Sowerberry. "Run to Mr Bumble, Noah, and tell him to come here directly, and not to lose a minute; never mind your cap; make haste!"

Noah started off at his fullest speed until he reached the workhouse-gate. Having rested here, for a minute or so, to collect a good burst of sobs and tears, he knocked loudly at the gate.

"Mr Bumble! Mr Bumble!" cried Noah so loudly that Mr Bumble, who happened to be near by, was alarmed, and rushed into the yard without his cocked hat.

"Oh, Mr Bumble, sir!" said Noah. "Oliver, sir— Oliver has——"

"What? What?" interrupted Mr Bumble; "not run away; he hasn't run away, has he, Noah?"

"No, sir, no. Not run away, sir, but he's turned fierce," replied Noah. "He tried to murder me, sir, and then tried to murder Charlotte, and then Missis. Oh! What a dreadful pain, sir!" And here Noah twisted his body like a snake, thus giving Mr Bumble the impression that he was suffering from the terrible savage attack of Oliver.

Mr Bumble, adjusting his cocked hat and taking his cane, accompanied Noah Claypole with all speed to the undertaker's shop.

Sowerberry had not returned, and Oliver continued to kick at the cellar door. Mr Bumble gave a kick at the outside and then, applying his mouth to the keyhole, said in a deep impressive tone:

"Oliver!"

"Come, you let me out!" replied Oliver from the inside.

"Do you know this voice, Oliver?" said Mr Bumble.

"Yes," replied Oliver.

"Aren't you afraid of it, sir? Aren't you trembling while I speak, sir?" said Mr Bumble.

"No!" replied Oliver boldly.

Mr Bumble stepped back from the keyhole; drew himself up to his full height; and looked from one to another of those standing by, in silent astonishment.

"Oh, you know, Mr Bumble, he must be mad," said Mrs Sowerberry. "No boy in half his senses would dare to speak so to you."

"It's not madness, ma'am," replied Mr Bumble, after a moment's deep thinking. "It's meat."

"What?" exclaimed Mrs Sowerberry.

"Meat, ma'am, meat," replied Mr Bumble. "You've overfed him, ma'am. If you had kept the boy on soup, ma'am, this would never have happened."

"Dear, dear!" exclaimed Mrs Sowerberry. "This comes of being generous!"

"Ah!" said Mr Bumble, "the only thing that can be done now is to leave him in the cellar for a day or so, till he's starved down; and to take him out, and keep him on soup all through his apprenticeship. He comes of a bad family, Mrs Sowerberry! Both the nurse and the doctor said that his mother had made her way here against difficulties and pain that would have killed any good woman weeks before."

At this point of Mr Bumble's speech, Oliver, just hearing enough to know that some new reference was being made to his mother, re-started kicking violently. At this moment Sowerberry returned. Oliver's offence having been explained to him with such exaggeration as the ladies thought would rouse his anger, he unlocked the cellar-door and dragged Oliver out by the collar.

Oliver's clothes had been torn in the beating he had received: his face was bruised and scratched; and his hair was scattered over his forehead. But the angry colour had not disappeared, and when he was pulled out of his prison he looked at Noah quite unafraid.

"Now, you're a nice young fellow, aren't you?" said Sowerberry, giving Oliver a shake, and a box on the ear.

"He called my mother names," replied Oliver.

"Well, and what if he did, you little ungrateful wretch?" said Mrs Sowerberry. "She deserved what he said, and worse."

"She didn't," said Oliver.

"She did," said Mrs Sowerberry.

"It's a lie," said Oliver.

Mrs Sowerberry burst into a flood of tears.

This flood of tears left Mr Sowerberry no choice; so he at once gave Oliver a good beating, which satisfied even Mrs Sowerberry herself and rendered Mr Bumble's use of the cane, which followed, rather unnecessary. For the rest of the day, he was shut up in the back kitchen and at night Mrs Sowerberry ordered him upstairs to his miserable bed.

It was not until he was left alone in the silence of the gloomy workshop of the undertaker that Oliver gave way to his feelings. He had listened to their insults with contempt, and he had endured the whip without a cry. But now, when there were none to see or hear him, he fell upon his knees on the floor and, hiding his face in his hands, he wept such tears, as, please God, few so young may ever have cause to pour out.

For a long time Oliver remained motionless in this position. The candle was burning low when he rose to his feet. Having gazed cautiously around him, and listened intently, he gently undid the fastenings of the door, and looked outside.

It was a cold, dark night. There was no wind, and the dark shadows thrown by the trees upon the ground looked fearful. He closed the door again, tied up the few articles of clothing he had, and sat down upon a bench, to wait for morning.

With the first ray of light that struggled through the shutters, Oliver rose, and again unfastened the door. One timid look—one moment's hesitation—he had closed it behind him and was in the open street.

Chapter 6

The Artful Dodger

By eight o'clock Oliver was nearly five miles away from the town, but he ran and hid behind the hedges by turns, till noon, lest he should be pursued and overtaken. Then he sat down to rest by the side of a milestone and began to think, for the first time, where he had better go and try to live.

The milestone told him, in big letters, that he was now

seventy miles from London. The name awakened a new train of ideas in his mind. London!—that great large place!—nobody—not even Mr Bumble—could ever find him there! He had often heard the old men in the workhouse, too, say that no lad of spirit would find it difficult to earn his living in London. As these thoughts passed through his mind, he jumped upon his feet and again walked forward.

Oliver walked twenty miles that day; and all that time tasted nothing but a crust of dry bread. When night came, he turned into a meadow, and creeping under a hay-rick he lay there and soon fell asleep.

He felt cold and stiff when he got up the next morning, and so hungry that he was obliged to spend the only penny he had on a small loaf. Another night passed in the cold, damp air made him worse, and when he set forward on his journey next morning, he could hardly crawl along.

He continued in this manner for six days, begging at cottage doors in the villages where it was not forbidden to beg. Early on the seventh morning after he had left his native place, he walked slowly and painfully into the little town of Barnet. The window shutters were closed; the streets were empty; not a soul had awakened to the business of the day. The sun was rising in all its splendid beauty; but the light only served to show the boy his loneliness as he sat, with bleeding feet and covered with dust, upon a doorstep.

By degrees the shutters were opened; the window-blinds were drawn up; and people began passing to and fro.

He had been sitting on the doorstep for some time when he observed that a boy, who had passed him carelessly some minutes before, had returned and was now looking at him closely from the opposite side of the way. Presently the boy crossed over and walking close up to Oliver said:

"Hullo! What's the trouble?"

The boy who addressed Oliver in this manner was about his own age, but one of the strangest looking boys Oliver had ever seen. He was a dirty little boy, but he had about him all the manners of a man. He was short for his age, with little sharp, ugly eyes. His hat was stuck on the top of his head so lightly, that it threatened to fall off every moment. He wore a man's coat, which reached nearly to his heels. He had turned the cuffs back, halfway up the arms, to get his hands out of the sleeves, apparently with the purpose of thrusting them into his trouser pockets, for there he kept them. He was, altogether, as bold and boastful a young gentleman as ever stood four feet six, or something less.

"Hullo, my boy! What's the trouble?" said this strange young gentleman to Oliver.

"I am very hungry and tired," replied Oliver, the tears standing in his eyes as he spoke. "I have walked a long way. I have been walking these seven days."

"Walking for seven days!" said the young gentleman. "You want some food, and you shall have it. I am a poor boy myself, but I have a shilling and I'll pay. Get up and come with me."

Helping Oliver to rise, this young man took him to a neighbouring shop, where he bought him some ham and a big loaf of bread. Then he took him to a small public-house where a pot of beer was brought to him, and he made a long and hearty meal.

"Going to London?" said the strange boy, when Oliver had at length finished his meal.

"Yes."

"Got any lodgings?"

"No."

"Money?"

"No."

The strange boy whistled, and put his arms into his

19

pockets as far as the big coat sleeves would let them go.

"Do you live in London?" inquired Oliver.

"Yes, I do, when I'm at home," replied the boy. "I suppose you want some place to sleep in tonight, don't you?"

"I do indeed," answered Oliver. "I have not slept under a roof since I left the country."

"Don't cry," said the young gentleman. "I've got to be in London tonight; and I know a respectable old gentleman who lives there, and he'll give you lodgings for nothing, if any gentleman he knows introduces you. And he knows me very well."

This unexpected offer of shelter was too tempting to be resisted; especially as it was immediately followed up by the assurance that the old gentleman would provide Oliver with a comfortable job, without loss of time. This led to a more friendly conversation between the two boys, from which Oliver discovered that his friend's name was Jack Dawkins, but that among his intimate friends he was called "The Artful Dodger".

As Jack Dawkins objected to their entering London before nightfall, it was nearly eleven o'clock when they reached the outskirts. They passed through one of the ugliest and dirtiest parts of London until at last, they reached the bottom of a hill. Oliver was considering whether he hadn't better run away, but the Dodger, catching him by the arm, pushed open the door of a house, and drawing him into the passage, closed it behind him.

He gave a whistle and the light of a candle gleamed on the wall at the end of the passage; and a man's face peeped out.

"There's two of you," said the man, shading his eyes with his hand. "Who's the other one?"

"A new friend," replied Jack Dawkins, pulling Oliver forward. "Is Fagin upstairs?"

"Yes, he's sorting the handkerchiefs, up with you!"
The candle was drawn back, and the face disappeared.

Oliver, groping his way with one hand, and having the other firmly grasped by his companion, ascended with much difficulty the dark and broken stairs. Jack Dawkins threw open the door of a back room and drew Oliver after him.

The walls and ceiling of the room were perfectly black with age and dirt. There was a wooden table before the fire, upon which were a candle, stuck in a beer bottle, two or three cups, a loaf and butter, and a plate. In a frying-pan on the fire some sausages were cooking; and standing over them was a very old Jew, whose evil-looking face was partly hidden by his thick, red hair. He was dressed in a greasy woollen gown, with his throat bare, and he seemed to be dividing his attention between the frying-pan and a number of silk handkerchiefs which were hanging over a line. Several rough beds made of old sacks were laid side by side on the floor. Seated round the table were four or five boys, none older than the Dodger, smoking long clay pipes, and drinking spirits with the air of middle-aged men. These crowded round the Dodger as he whispered a few words to the Jew, and then turned round and looked at Oliver. So did the Jew himself.

"This is him, Fagin," said the Dodger; "my friend, Oliver Twist."

The Jew smiled, and making a low bow to Oliver, took him by the hand and hoped he should have the honour of his friendship. Upon this the young gentlemen with the pipes came round him, and shook both his hands very hard especially the one in which he held his little bundle.

"We are very glad to see you, Oliver," said the Jew. "Dodger, take off the sausages; and draw a chair near the fire for Oliver. Ah, you're looking at the handkerchiefs, eh, my dear? There are a good many of them, aren't there? We've just sorted them out, ready for the wash; that's all, Oliver; that's all. Ha! ha! ha! "

The latter part of his speech was met by a loud shout from all the pupils of the merry old gentleman, and they all went to supper.

Chapter 7

Fagin the Jew and his band

It was late next morning when Oliver awoke. There was no other person in the room but the old Jew, who was making himself some coffee for breakfast and whistling softly to himself as he stirred it round and round.

Although Oliver had roused himself from sleep he was not thoroughly awake; he was in a drowsy state, between sleeping and waking. He saw the Jew with his half-closed eyes and heard his low whistling.

When the coffee was ready the Jew stood for a few minutes as if he did not know how to employ himself, then he turned round and looked at Oliver, and called him by his name. He did not answer and was to all appearances asleep. The Jew now stepped gently to the door and fastened it. He then drew out from some secret hole in the floor, a small box which he placed carefully on the table. His eyes shone as he raised the lid, and looked in. Dragging an old chair to the table, he sat down and took out from the box a magnificent gold watch, sparkling with jewels.

"Ah!" said the Jew, smiling to himself in an ugly manner. "Clever dogs! Faithful to the last! Never informed about old Fagin! And why should they? It wouldn't have saved them from hanging. No, no, no! Fine fellows! Fine fellows!"

With these, and other similar reflections, the Jew replaced the watch in its place of safety. At least half a dozen more were drawn out, one by one from the same box, and examined with equal pleasure, besides rings, brooches, bracelets, and other articles of jewellery of fine workmanship.

As the Jew murmured to himself, his dark eyes fell on Oliver's face; the boy's eyes were fixed on his in silent curiosity, and the Jew realised that he had been observed. He closed the lid of the box with a loud crash; and, laying his hand on a bread knife which was on the table, started up furiously.

"What's that?" said the Jew. "What do you watch me for? Why are you awake? What have you seen? Speak out, boy! Quick—quick! for your life!"

"I wasn't able to sleep any longer, sir," replied Oliver. "I am sorry if I have disturbed you, sir."

"So you were not awake an hour ago?" said the Jew, looking fiercely at the boy.

"No! No! indeed!" replied Oliver.

"Are you sure?" cried the Jew, with a still fiercer look than before, and a threatening attitude.

"Upon my word I was not, sir," replied Oliver earnestly. "I was not, indeed, sir."

"It's all right, my dear," said the Jew, suddenly changing his tone and resuming his old manner, and playing with the knife a little, before he laid it down, as if to make Oliver think that he had picked it up in mere sport. "Of course I know that, my dear. I only tried to frighten you. You're a brave boy. Ha! ha! you're a brave boy, Oliver!" The Jew rubbed his hands as he laughed, but looked uneasily at the box.

"Did you see any of these pretty things, my dear?" said the Jew, laying his hand upon it after a short pause.

"Yes, sir," replied Oliver.

"Ah!" said the Jew, turning rather pale. "They—they're mine, Oliver; my little property. All I have to live upon, in my old age. People call me a miser, my dear. Only a miser, that's all."

Oliver thought the old man must be a decided miser to live in such a dirty place with so many watches. He asked the Jew if he might get up.

"Certainly, my dear, certainly," replied the old gentleman. "Wait. There's a jug of water in the corner by the door. Bring it here and I'll give you a basin to wash in, my dear."

Oliver got up, walked across the room and bent for an instant to raise the jug, and when he turned his head, the box was gone.

He had scarcely washed himself when the Dodger returned, accompanied by a very active young friend, whom Oliver had seen smoking on the previous night, and who was now introduced to him as Charlie Bates. The four sat down to breakfast on the coffee and some hot rolls and ham which the Dodger had brought with him inside his hat.

"Well," said the Jew, glancing cunningly at Oliver, and addressing himself to the Dodger, "I hope you've been at work this morning, my dears?"

"Hard," replied the Dodger.

"As nails," added Charlie Bates.

"Good boys, good boys!" said the Jew. "What have you got, Dodger?"

"A couple of pocket-books," replied that young gentleman.

"Lined?" inquired the Jew, eagerly.

"Pretty well," said the Dodger, producing his pocket-books.

"Not so heavy as they might be," said the Jew, after looking at the insides carefully; "but very neat and nicely made. A clever workman, isn't he, Oliver?"

"Very, indeed, sir," said Oliver. At which Mr Charlie Bates laughed noisily; very much to the amazement of Oliver, who saw nothing to laugh at.

"And what have you got, my dear?" said Fagin to Charlie Bates.

"Handkerchiefs," replied Master Bates, producing four.

"Well," said the Jew, examining them closely; "they're very good ones. But you haven't marked them well, Charlie; so the marks shall be picked out with a needle, and we'll teach Oliver how to do it. Shall we, Oliver? Ha! ha! ha!"

"If you please, sir," said Oliver.

"You'd like to be able to make pocket-handkerchiefs as easily as Charlie Bates, wouldn't you, my dear?" said the Jew.

"Very much indeed, if you'll teach me, sir," replied Oliver.

Master Bates saw something so funny in this reply that he burst into another laugh which nearly choked him.

"He's so very green!" he said, when he recovered.

When the breakfast was cleared away, the merry old gentleman and the two boys played at a very uncommon game, which was performed in this way: the merry old gentleman put a snuff-box in one pocket of his trousers, a pocket-book in the other, and a watch in his waistcoat pocket. He fastened a false diamond pin in his shirt, and, buttoning his coat tightly round him, walked up and down the room with a stick, in imitation of the manner of an old man walking about the streets. Sometimes he stopped at the fire-place, and sometimes at the door, pretending that he was staring into shop windows. At such times, he would look around him for fear of thieves, and would keep slapping all his pockets in turn to see that he hadn't lost anything. He did this in such a funny manner that Oliver laughed till the tears ran down his face. All this time the two boys followed him closely about, getting out of his sight so quickly, every time he turned round, that it was impossible to follow their movements. At last the Dodger trod upon his toes accidentally, while Charlie Bates stumbled up against him behind and in that one moment they took from him, with most extraordinary speed, snuff-box, pocket-book, shirt-pin, pocket-handkerchief, even the spectacle-case. If the old gentleman felt a hand in any one of the pockets, he cried out where it was; and the game began all over again.

When this game had been played a great many times, a couple of young ladies, one of whom was named Bet, and the other Nancy, called to see the young gentlemen. They were untidily dressed, and not exactly pretty, but they were very free and agreeable in their manners and Oliver thought them very nice indeed.

These visitors stayed a long time, drinking spirits and talking gaily. At last they went out, accompanied by Charlie Bates and the Dodger, having been provided by the good old Jew with money to spend.

"There, my dear," said Fagin, "that's a pleasant life, isn't it? Make these young gentlemen your models, and take their advice in all matters—especially the Dodger's, my dear. He'll be a great man himself, and will make you one too, if you follow his example. Is my handkerchief hanging out of my pocket, my dear?" said the Jew.

"Yes, sir," said Oliver.

"See if you can take it out, without my feeling it, as you saw them do, when we were at play this morning."

Oliver held out the bottom of the pocket with one hand, as he had seen the Dodger hold it; and drew the handkerchief lightly out with the other hand.

"Is it gone?" cried the Jew.

"Here it is, sir," said Oliver, showing it in his hand.

"You're a clever boy, my dear," said the playful old gentleman, patting Oliver on the head approvingly. "I never saw a sharper lad. Here's a shilling for you. If you go on in this way you'll be a great man. And now come here; I'll show you how to take the marks out of the handkerchiefs."

Oliver wondered how picking the old gentleman's pocket would make him a great man. But thinking that the old Jew must know best, he followed him quietly to the table and was soon deeply engaged in his new study.

Chapter 8

Oliver is arrested

For many days, Oliver remained in the Jew's room, picking the marks out of the handkerchiefs, and sometimes taking part in the game already described. At last he began to feel the need for fresh air and begged the old gentleman to allow him to go out to work with his two companions.

Finally the old Jew granted him his request and the three boys went out. At first they walked at such a slow pace that Oliver began to think that his companions were not going to work at all. But suddenly, just as they were coming out of a narrow street, the Dodger stopped and drew his companions back with the greatest caution.

"What's the matter?" demanded Oliver.

"Hush!" replied the Dodger. "Do you see that old *r* at the bookshop?"

"The old gentleman across the street?" said Oliver. "Yes, I see him."

"He'll do," said the Dodger.

"A first class chance," observed Charlie Bates.

Oliver looked from one to the other, with the greatest surprise; but he was not permitted to make any inquiries; for the two boys walked stealthily across the road, closely following the old gentleman. Oliver walked a few steps after them; and, not knowing whether to advance or retreat, stood looking on in silent amazement.

The old gentleman was a very respectable looking person, with a powdered head and gold spectacles. He had taken up a book from the shelf inside the bookshop and there stood, reading as hard as if it were his own study. He was so intent on reading that he saw neither shop, nor street, nor boys; he saw nothing but the book he was reading.

Imagine Oliver's horror and alarm to see the Dodger thrust his hand into the old gentleman's pocket, and draw from it a handkerchief! To see him hand this to Charlie Bates, and finally to see them both running away round the corner at full speed.

In an instant the whole mystery of the handkerchiefs, and the watches, and the jewels, and the Jew rushed upon the boy's mind. He stood terrified and confused for a moment, and then he ran away as fast as his legs could carry him.

This was all done in a minute's space. At the very instant when Oliver began to run away, the old gentleman, putting his hand in his pocket and missing his handkerchief, turned sharply round. Seeing Oliver run away at such a rapid pace, he very naturally concluded that he was the robber and, shouting "Stop Thief!" with all his might, ran after him, book in hand.

The Dodger and Bates, hearing the cry and seeing

Oliver running, guessed exactly how the matter stood; they stopped running away, and shouting "Stop thief!" too, they joined in the pursuit like good citizens.

"Stop thief! Stop thief!" There is a magic in the sound. The cry is taken up by a hundred voices, and the crowd of pursuers increases at every step and turning. Away they fly, splashing through the mud, and rattling along the pavements.

There is a passion for hunting something deeply fixed in the human breast. One wretched, breathless child, with terror in his eyes; large drops of sweat streaming down his face; his pursuers follow on his track, and gain upon him every instant.

Stopped at last! A clever blow. He is down on the pavement, and the crowd gathers eagerly round him, each newcomer struggling with the others to catch a glimpse. "Stand aside!" "Give him a little air!" "Nonsense! he doesn't deserve it." "Here is the gentleman. Is this the boy, sir?" "Yes."

Oliver lay, covered with mud and dust, and bleeding from the mouth, looking wildly round upon the faces that surrounded him, when the old gentleman was pushed into the circle by the foremost of the pursuers.

"Yes," said the gentleman, "I am afraid it is the boy. Poor fellow! He has hurt himself."

"*I* did it, sir," said a great big fellow, stepping forward; "*I* stopped him, sir."

The fellow touched his hat with a smile, expecting something for his trouble; but the old gentleman looked at him with an expression of dislike, and would have run away himself had not a police officer at that moment made his way through the crowd and seized Oliver by the collar.

"Come, get up," said the officer roughly.

"It wasn't me, indeed, sir. It was two other boys," said

Oliver, joining his hands passionately and looking round. "They are here somewhere."

"Oh, no, they aren't," said the officer; "come, get up!"

"Don't hurt him," said the old gentleman pitifully.

"Oh no, I won't hurt him," replied the officer, tearing Oliver's jacket half off his back. "Come, I know you; it won't do. Will you stand upon your feet, you young devil?"

Oliver, who could hardly stand, was dragged along the street by the coat collar, at a rapid pace. The gentleman walked on with them by the officer's side; and many of the people in the crowd got a little ahead and stared back at Oliver from time to time. The boys shouted in triumph, and on they went.

Chapter 9

Oliver is released

Oliver and the old gentleman were taken to the office of the magistrate, Mr Fang; a thin, stern, hot-tempered man who was in the habit of drinking more than was good for him.

The old gentleman bowed respectfully and, advancing to the magistrate's desk, put his card on it, saying:

"That's my name and address, sir." But the magistrate was out of temper; he looked up angrily from the newspaper he was reading.

"Who are you?" said Mr Fang.

The old gentleman pointed, with some surprise, to the card.

"Officer!" said Mr Fang, tossing the card contemptuously away. "Who is this fellow?"

"My name, sir," said the old gentleman, "is Brownlow. Permit me to inquire the name of the magistrate who insults a respectable person under the protection of the bench."

"Officer!" said Mr Fang, "what's this fellow charged with?"

"He's not charged at all, your worship," replied the officer. "He appears against the boy, your worship."

"Appears against the boy, does he?" said Mr Fang, looking contemptuously at Mr Brownlow from head to foot. "Swear him!"

"Before I am sworn, I must beg to say one word," said Mr Brownlow; "and that is, that I really never, without actual experience, could have believed——"

"Hold your tongue, sir!" said Mr Fang.

"I will not, sir!" replied the old gentleman.

"Hold your tongue this instant, or I'll have you turned out of the office!" said Mr Fang. "Swear this person!" he added to the clerk.

Mr Brownlow's anger was roused; but reflecting perhaps that he might only injure the boy by expressing his anger, he suppressed his feelings and submitted to be sworn at once.

"Now," said Mr Fang, "what's the charge against the boy? What have you got to say, sir?"

"I was standing at a bookshop——" Mr Brownlow began.

"Hold your tongue, sir," said Mr Fang. "Policeman! Where's the policeman? Here, swear this policeman. Now, policeman, what is this?"

The policeman humbly related how he had arrested Oliver, and how he had searched him and found nothing on his person.

"Are there any witnesses?" inquired Mr Fang.

"None, your worship," replied the policeman.

Mr Fang sat silent for some minutes, and then, turning round angrily to Mr Brownlow, he said:

"Do you mean to state your complaint against this boy, or do you not? You have been sworn. Now, if you stand there refusing to give evidence I'll punish you for disrespect of the court."

With many interruptions, and repeated insults, Mr Brownlow managed to state his case; observing that, in the surprise of the moment, he had run after the boy because he saw him running away. He begged the magistrate to deal as gently with him as justice would allow.

"He has been hurt already," said the old gentleman in conclusion. "And I fear," he added, "that he is ill."

"Oh, yes, I dare say!" said Mr Fang, mockingly. "Come, none of your tricks here, you young rascal; they won't do. What's your name?"

Oliver tried to reply, but his tongue failed him. He was deadly pale; and the whole place seemed to be turning round and round.

The officer being a kind-hearted man and seeing that Oliver was too weak and afraid to answer for himself, answered the magistrate's questions and told him that he thought the boy was really ill.

But the magistrate sentenced him to three months' imprisonment, with hard labour, and the boy would have been taken away to prison had it not been for the owner of the bookshop, who rushed hastily into the office and advanced towards the bench.

"Stop! Stop! Don't take him away! For heaven's sake stop a moment!" cried the newcomer, breathless with haste.

"What's this? Who is this man? Turn this man out. Clear the office!" cried Mr Fang.

"I *will* speak," cried the man; "I will not be turned out. I saw it all. I keep the bookshop. I demand to be sworn."

"Swear the man," growled Mr Fang. "Now, man, what have you got to say?"

The bookseller related how he had seen the three boys, the prisoner and two others, loitering on the opposite side of the road, when Mr Brownlow was reading. He said that the robbery had been committed by another boy; that Oliver was perfectly amazed by it.

Having listened to his story the magistrate ordered the boy to be released and the office to be cleared.

A coach was obtained and Oliver having been carefully laid on one seat, the old gentleman got in and sat on the other, and away the coach drove to Mr Brownlow's house.

Chapter 10

Oliver stays at Mr Brownlow's

At Mr Brownlow's house a bed was quickly prepared for Oliver and he was carefully and comfortably laid in it; here he was looked after with a kindness that knew no bounds.

But for many days Oliver remained insensible to all the goodness of his new friends. He lay on his bed wasting away under the heat of fever. When at last he awoke from what seemed to have been a long and troubled dream he was weak, thin and pale. Raising himself in the bed, with his head resting on his trembling arm, he looked anxiously around.

"What room is this? Where have I been brought?" said Oliver. "This is not the place I went to sleep in."

A motherly old lady who had been sitting at the bed-side rose as she heard these words and said to him softly:

"Hush, my dear. You must be very quiet, or you will be ill again. Lie down again; there's a dear!"

Oliver obeyed, partly to please the old lady, who was so kind to him, and partly because he was still very weak. He soon fell into a gentle sleep, from which he was awakened by the light of a candle, to see a doctor feel his pulse and hear him say that he was a great deal better.

The doctor told Mrs Bedwin, the kind old lady, to give him a little tea and some toast, not to keep him too warm or too cold, and then he went away.

Oliver fell asleep again; when he woke it had been a bright day for hours; he felt cheerful and happy. The most dangerous part of the disease had passed. He belonged to the world again. In three days' time he was able to sit in an easy chair, and as he was still too weak to walk, Mrs Bedwin had him carried downstairs to her room, where she set him by the fireside and sat beside him.

The old gentleman, Mr Brownlow, came to see him. "How do you feel, my dear?" he said.

"Very happy, sir," said Oliver. "And very grateful indeed, sir, for your goodness to me."

"Good boy," said Mr Brownlow. "Have you given him any food, Mrs Bedwin?"

"He has just had a basin of beautiful strong soup, sir," she replied.

After a few more questions and a little conversation with Oliver Mr Brownlow went away.

They were happy days, those of Oliver's recovery. Everything was so quiet, and neat, and orderly. Everybody was kind and gentle. He was no sooner strong enough to put his clothes on than Mr Brownlow caused a complete new suit, a new cap and a new pair of shoes to be provided for him.

One evening Mr Brownlow sent for Oliver to come and

talk to him in his study. Oliver was admitted into a little room, quite full of books. Mr Brownlow was seated at a table, reading. When he saw Oliver he pushed the book away from him, and told him to come near the table and sit down. Oliver did so and surveyed with curiosity the book-shelves that reached from the floor to the ceiling.

"There are a good many books, are there not, my boy?" said Mr Brownlow.

"A great number, sir," replied Oliver. "I never saw so many."

"You shall read them, if you behave well," said the old gentleman kindly; "and you will like that, better than looking at the outside. How would you like to grow up a clever man and write books?"

"I think I would rather read them, sir," replied Oliver.

"Now," said Mr Brownlow in a more serious manner, "I want you to pay great attention, my boy, to what I am going to say. I shall talk to you without any reserve, because I am sure you are as well able to understand me as many older persons would be."

"Oh, don't tell me you are going to send me away, sir, please!" exclaimed Oliver, alarmed at the serious tone of Mr Brownlow. "Don't turn me out of doors to wander in the streets again. Let me stay here and be a servant. Don't send me back to the wretched place I came from. Have mercy upon a poor boy, sir!"

"My dear child," said the old gentleman, moved by the warmth of Oliver's sudden appeal; "you need not be afraid of my deserting you, unless you give me cause."

"I never, never will, sir," said Oliver.

"I hope not," said the old gentleman. "I do not think you ever will. I feel strongly inclined to trust you. You say you are an orphan, without a friend in the world; all the inquiries I have been able to make confirm this statement. Let me hear your story; where you came from; who brought you up; and how you got into the company in which I found you. Speak the truth, and you shall not be friendless while I live."

Oliver began to tell his sad story. While he was doing so an old friend of Mr Brownlow, called Mr Grimwig, arrived. Mr Grimwig was a stout old gentleman, rather lame in one leg, and he walked supported by a thick stick. He had a manner of twisting his head on one side when he spoke; and of looking out of the corners of his eyes at the same time, which reminded one of a parrot. In this attitude he fixed himself, the moment he made his appearance; and holding out a small piece of orange-peel at arm's length, he exclaimed in a growling, discontented voice:

"Look here! Do you see this! Isn't it a most extra-ordinary thing that I can't call at a friend's house but I find a piece of this surgeon's friend on the staircase? I've been lamed with orange-peel once and I know orange-peel will be my death, or I'll be content to eat my own head, sir!"

This was Mr Grimwig's peculiar manner of confirming nearly every statement he made.

"I'll eat my head, sir," repeated Mr Grimwig, striking his stick upon the ground. "Hallo! What's that?" looking at Oliver and retreating a step or two.

"This is young Oliver Twist, whom we were speaking about," said Mr Brownlow.

Oliver bowed.

"You don't mean to say that's the boy who had the fever, I hope?" said Mr Grimwig, drawing back a little. "Wait a minute! Don't speak! Stop——" continued Mr Grimwig, losing all dread of the fever in his triumph at the discovery; "that's the boy who had the orange! If that's not the boy, sir, who had the orange and threw this bit of peel upon the staircase, I'll eat my head and his too."

"No, no, he has not had one," said Mr Brownlow,

laughing. "Come! put down your hat, and speak to my young friend."

"I feel strongly on this subject, sir," said the old gentleman. "There's always orange peel on the pavement in our street; and I *know* it's put there by the surgeon's boy at the corner."

Then, putting on his eye-glasses, he looked at Oliver who, seeing that he was the object of inspection, coloured and bowed again.

"That's the boy, is it?" said Mr Grimwig, at length.

"That is the boy," replied Mr Brownlow.

"How are you, boy?" said Mr Grimwig.

"A great deal better, thank you, sir," replied Oliver.

Mr Brownlow asked Oliver to step downstairs and tell Mrs Bedwin they were ready for tea.

"He is a nice-looking boy, is he not?" inquired Mr Brownlow.

"I don't know," replied Mr Grimwig. "Where does he come from? Who is he? What is he? He has had a fever. What of that? Fevers are not peculiar to good people, are they?"

Now, the fact was that in his own heart Mr Grimwig was strongly disposed to admit that Oliver was a nice-looking and good-mannered boy; but he was very fond of contradiction. Mr Brownlow, knowing his friend's peculiarities, bore his opposition with good humour. And so matters went very smoothly at tea, and Oliver, who made one of the party, began to feel more at ease.

"And when are you going to hear a full and true account of the life and adventures of Oliver Twist?" asked Mr Grimwig of Mr Brownlow, at the end of the meal, looking sideways at Oliver.

"Tomorrow morning," replied Mr Brownlow. "I would rather he was alone with me at the time. Come up to see me tomorrow morning at ten o'clock, Oliver."

"Yes, sir," replied Oliver. He answered with some hesitation, because he was confused by Mr Grimwig's looking hard at him.

"I'll tell you what," whispered the gentleman to Mr Brownlow, "he won't come up to you tomorrow morning. I saw him hesitate. He is deceiving you, my good friend."

"I'll swear he is not," replied Mr Brownlow, warmly.

"If he is not," said Mr Grimwig, "I'll eat my head."

"We shall see," said Mr Brownlow, checking his rising anger.

"We will," replied Mr Grimwig, with an annoying smile; "we will."

As fate would have it, Mrs Bedwin chanced to bring in, at this moment, a small parcel of books which Mr Brownlow had that morning bought at the same bookshop in front of which his pocket had been picked.

"Stop the shop-boy, Mrs Bedwin!" said Mr Brownlow; "there is something to go back." But the boy had gone.

"Send Oliver with the books," said Mr Grimwig, with an ironical smile; "he will be sure to deliver them safely, you know."

"Yes; do let me take them, if you please, sir," said Oliver. "I'll run all the way, sir."

"You shall go, my dear," said the old man. "The books are on a chair by my table. Fetch them down."

Oliver, delighted to be of use, brought the books down and waited to hear what message he was to take.

"You are to say," said Mr Brownlow, looking steadily at Grimwig, "you are to say that you have brought those books back; and that you have come to pay the four pounds ten I owe them. This is a five-pound note, so you will have to bring me back ten shillings change."

"I won't be ten minutes, sir," said Oliver, and having buttoned up the bank-note in his coat pocket, and placed the books carefully under his arm, he made a respectful bow, and left the room. Mrs Bedwin followed him to the door, giving him many directions about the nearest way, and the name of the book-seller, and the name of the street; all of which Oliver said he clearly understood. Having told him to be sure and not take cold, the old lady at length permitted him to depart.

"Bless his sweet face!" said the old lady, looking after him. "I can't bear, somehow, to let him go out of my sight."

At this moment, Oliver looked gaily round, and nodded before he turned the corner. The old lady smilingly returned his nod, and, closing the door, went back to her own room.

"Let me see; he'll be back in twenty minutes at the longest," said Mr Brownlow, pulling out his watch and placing it on the table. "It will be dark by that time."

"Oh! you really expect him to come back, do you?" inquired Mr Grimwig.

"Don't you?" asked Mr Brownlow, smiling.

The spirit of contradiction was strong in Mr Grimwig's breast, at the moment; and it was rendered stronger by his friend's confident smile.

"No," he said, hitting the table with his fist. "I do not. The boy has a new suit of clothes on his back, a set of valuable books under his arm, and a five-pound note in his pocket. He'll join his old friends the thieves, and laugh at you. If ever that boy returns to this house, sir, I'll eat my head."

With these words he drew his chair closer to the table; and there the two friends sat in silent expectation, with the watch between them. It grew dark so that the figures on the watch face could scarcely be seen, but there the two gentlemen continued to sit, in silence, with the watch between them.

Chapter 11

In Fagin's hands once more

"Where's Oliver?" said the Jew, rising with a threatening look on seeing the Dodger and Charlie Bates without him. "Where's the boy?"

The young thieves looked uneasily at each other, but they made no reply.

"What's become of the boy?" said the Jew, seizing the Dodger tightly by the coat collar, and shaking him. "Speak out, or I'll strangle you!"

"Why, the police have got him, and that's all about it," said the Dodger angrily. "Come, let go of me, will you!" and pulling himself violently out of the big coat, which he left in the Jew's hand, the Dodger snatched up the toasting fork and would have thrust it into the Jew's breast had not the latter stepped back in time. Then, seizing up a pot of beer, Fagin prepared to throw it at the Dodger's head, but the Dodger avoiding the pot in time, the beer hit another member of the gang who had just arrived.

It was Bill Sikes, followed by his dog. Bill was a strongly built fellow of about thirty-five years of age with an angry-looking face and a beard of three days' growth.

"Who threw that beer at me? It is well it is the beer, and not the pot which hit me, or I'd have killed somebody. I might have known that nobody but a rich, plundering old Jew could afford to throw away any drink but water. What is it all about, Fagin? What are you up to? Ill-treating the boys, you greedy old thief? I wonder they don't murder you. I would, if I was in their place."

"Hush! hush! Mr Sikes," said the Jew, trembling; "don't speak so loud."

"None of your mistering," replied the ruffian; "you

always mean mischief when you call me mister. You know my name: out with it."

"Well, well, then—Bill Sikes," said the Jew humbly. "You seem out of humour, Bill."

"Perhaps I am," replied Sikes, and then he demanded a glass of spirits; "and mind you don't poison it," he added, putting his hat on the table.

The young robbers told Sikes how Oliver Twist had been captured and how the police had arrested him.

"I'm afraid," said the Jew, "that he may say something which may get us into trouble."

"That's very likely," returned Sikes.

"And I'm afraid, you see," added the Jew, "that if the game was up with us, it might be up with a good many more, and that it would come out rather worse for you than it would for me, my dear."

"Somebody must find out what has happened at the magistrate's office," said Sikes. "If he hasn't informed, and is found guilty, there's no fear till he comes out again, and then he must be taken care of. You must get hold of him somehow."

The Jew nodded assent.

The prudence of this line of action was obvious; but unfortunately neither the Jew, nor Sikes, nor the Dodger nor Bates had any desire to go near a police-station. Presently two young ladies entered whom Oliver had seen on a former occasion.

"The very thing!" said the Jew. "Bet will go; won't you, my dear?"

"Where?" inquired the young lady.

"Only just up to the magistrate's office, my dear," said the Jew.

Bet refused to go, and Fagin turned to Nancy.

"Nancy, my dear," he said, "what do you say?"

"That I shan't go either," said she.

"She'll go, Fagin," said Sikes.

And Mr Sikes was right. By alternate threats, promises and bribes Nancy was at last prevailed upon to accept the mission.

She made her way to the police-office and when she came to the police-officer she burst into tears and began to cry aloud, apparently in great distress, saying:

"Oh, my brother! What has become of him? Where have they taken him to? Oh! Do have pity and tell me what's been done with the dear boy, if you please, sir!"

The officer informed the deeply affected sister that Oliver had been taken ill in the office and released because a witness had proved the robbery to have been committed by another boy. He told her that the gentleman who had accused Oliver had carried him away to his own house, somewhere at Pentonville.

In a dreadful state of uncertainty the young woman walked to the gate, and then she ran as fast as she could, by the most complicated route she could think of, to the Jew's house.

Mr Bill Sikes no sooner heard her account than he called up his white dog and quickly departed.

Fagin instructed Nancy, Charlie and the Dodger to do nothing but loiter about until they brought home some news of him. He unlocked the drawer and gave them some money, telling them that he would shut up his house that night, and that they knew where to find him.

Then he pushed them from the room and, carefully locking and barring the door behind them, he drew from its hiding-place the box which Oliver had seen him examine. He hastily took out the watches and the jewellery and hiding them under his clothes, he left the house.

Oliver Twist was on his way to the bookshop. He was walking along, thinking how happy and contented he ought to feel, when he was startled by a young woman screaming out very loud, "Oh, my dear brother!" and he had hardly looked up, to see what the matter was, when he was stopped by having a pair of arms thrown tight around his neck.

"Don't!" said Oliver, struggling. "Let go of me. Who is it? What are you stopping me for?"

The only reply to this was a great number of loud screams from the young woman who had embraced him. They were answered by the arrival of a brutal-looking man, whom Nancy, for the young woman was she, addressed by the name of Bill Sikes. He was closely followed by a miserable dog.

Darkness had set in, it was a low neighbourhood; no help was near; resistance was useless. In another moment Oliver was dragged into a maze of dark, narrow streets, and was forced along them at such speed as made his cries useless.

Meanwhile, in Mr Brownlow's house, the gas-lamps were lighted; Mrs Bedwin was waiting anxiously at the open door; the servant had run up the streets twenty times to see if there were any traces of Oliver; and still the two old gentlemen sat, in the dark parlour, with the watch between them.

The narrow streets at length ended in a large open space. Having crossed that, Oliver's captors turned into a very dirty narrow street, nearly full of old-clothes shops. The dog ran forward and stopped before the door of a shop that was closed and apparently unoccupied; the house was in a poor state of repair and on the door was nailed a TO LET sign-board which looked as if it had hung there for many years.

"All right," cried Sikes, looking cautiously about.

Nancy bent below the shutters, and Oliver heard the

sound of a bell. They crossed to the opposite side of the street, and stood for a few moments under a lamp. A little window was gently opened; soon afterwards the door softly opened. Mr Sikes then seized the terrified boy by the collar, and all three were soon inside the house.

The passage was perfectly dark. They waited, while the person who had let them in chained and barred the door.

"Is Fagin here?" asked the robber.

"Yes," replied the voice; "won't he be glad to see you? Oh, no!"

The style of this reply, as well as the voice which uttered it, seemed familiar to Oliver's ears; in fact it was the Artful Dodger, who presently lit a candle and led them in. They crossed an empty kitchen, and, opening the door of a small back room, they were received with a shout of laughter.

"Oh, Fagin, look at him! Fagin, do look at him! I can't bear it; it is such a jolly game, I can't bear it. Hold me, somebody, while I laugh it out."

It was Master Bates who, unable to control his merriment, laid himself flat on the floor and laughed noisily for five minutes.

The Jew, taking off his nightcap, made a great number of low bows to the amazed boy. Meanwhile, the Artful was busy picking Oliver's pockets.

"Look at his suit, Fagin!" said Charlie Bates; "fine cloth and a swell cut. And his books, too! Nothing but a gentleman, Fagin!"

"Delighted to see you looking so well, my dear," said the Jew, bowing with mock humility. "The Artful shall give you another suit, my dear, for fear you should spoil that Sunday one. Why didn't you write, my dear, and say you were coming? We'd have got something warm for supper."

At this Master Bates roared again, so loud that Fagin himself relaxed, and even the Dodger smiled. At that instant the Dodger drew forth the five-pound note.

44

"Hallo! what's that?" inquired Sikes, stepping forward as the Jew seized the note. "That's mine, Fagin."

"No, no, my dear," said the Jew. "Mine, Bill, mine. You shall have the books."

"If that isn't mine," said Bill Sikes, putting on his hat with a determined air, "mine and Nancy's, that is, I'll take the boy back again."

The Jew started.

"Come! Hand it over, will you?" said Sikes.

"This is hardly fair, Bill; hardly fair, is it, Nancy?" inquired the Jew.

"Fair or not fair," replied Sikes, "hand over, I tell you. Do you think Nancy and me has got nothing else to do with our precious time but to spend it in capturing every young boy who gets caught through you? Give it here, you greedy old thief, give it here."

With these words Sikes snatched the note from between the Jew's finger and thumb, folded it up and tied it in his handkerchief. He told the Jew he might keep the books, if he was fond of reading; if not, he could sell them.

"They belong to the old gentleman," said Oliver; "to the kind old gentleman who took me into his house, and had me nursed when I was nearly dying of the fever. Oh, please send them back; send him back the books and money. He'll think I stole them; the old lady, too; she will think I stole them. Oh, do have mercy upon me, and send them back."

With these words Oliver fell upon his knees at the Jew's feet.

"The boy is right," remarked Fagin. "You're right, Oliver, you're right; they *will* think you have stolen them. Ha! ha! It couldn't have happened better, if we had chosen our time!"

"Of course it couldn't," replied Sikes; "I knew that as soon as I saw him coming with the books under his arm.

It's all right enough. They're soft-hearted people, or they wouldn't have taken him at all; and they'll ask no questions after him, lest they should be obliged to have him arrested and brought before a court of law. He's safe enough."

On hearing these words Oliver jumped suddenly to his feet and tore wildly from the room, uttering loud cries for help.

"Keep back the dog, Bill!" cried Nancy, jumping to the door and closing it, as the Jew and his two pupils rushed out in pursuit. "Keep back the dog; he'll tear the boy to pieces."

"Serve him right!" cried Sikes, struggling to free himself from the girl's grasp. "Stand off from me, or I'll split your head against the wall."

He pushed the girl from him to the farther end of the room, just as the Jew and the two boys returned, dragging Oliver among them.

"So you wanted to run away, my dear, did you?" said the Jew, taking up a short heavy stick which lay in a corner of the fireplace.

Oliver made no reply, but he watched the Jew's motions, and breathed quickly.

"Wanted to get help; called for the police, did you?" said the Jew, catching the boy by the arm. "We'll cure you of that, my young master."

He gave Oliver a hard blow on the shoulders with the stick, and was raising it for a second when the girl, rushing forward, snatched it from his hand and threw it violently into the fire.

"I won't stand by and see it done, Fagin," cried the girl. "You've got the boy, and what more would you have? Leave him alone—leave him alone—or I'll kill you."

"Why, Nancy!" said the Jew, "you're more clever than ever tonight. Ha! ha! my dear, you are acting beautifully."

"Am I?" said the girl. "Take care I don't overdo it.

46

You will be the worse for it, Fagin, if I do; and so I tell you in good time to keep clear of me."

"What do you mean by this?" said Sikes. "Do you know who you are, and what you are?"

"Oh, yes, I know all about it," replied the girl.

"Well, then, keep quiet," growled Sikes, "or I'll quiet you for a good long time to come. You're a nice one, to take up the humane side and make a friend of the boy!"

"God help me, I am!" cried the girl passionately, "and I wish I had been struck dead in the street before I had lent a hand in bringing him here. He's a thief, a liar, a devil, all that's bad, from this night forth. Isn't that enough for the old wretch, without blows?"

"Come, come," said the Jew, "we must have civil words; civil words."

"Civil words!" cried the girl, whose anger was frightful to see. "Civil words, you villain! Yes, you deserve them from me. I robbed for you when I was a child not half as old as this!" pointing to Oliver. "I have been in the same trade for twelve years, don't you know it? Speak out! Don't you know it?"

"Well, well," replied the Jew, "and if you have, it's your living!"

"Aye, it is!" returned the girl. "It is my living; and the cold, wet, dirty streets are my home; and you're the wretch that drove me to them long ago, and that'll keep me there, day and night, day and night, till I die!"

"I shall do you more harm than that," said the Jew, "if you say any more!"

The girl said nothing more, but tearing her hair and dress in a fit of passion, made such a rush at the Jew as would have left marks of her revenge upon him, had not her wrists been seized by Sikes at the right moment. She struggled in vain, and then she fainted.

Chapter 12

Oliver is to take part in a robbery

About noon next day, when the Dodger and Bates had gone out, Mr Fagin gave Oliver a long lecture on the ungratefulness he showed in trying to run away from his friends. He told him how he had taken him in and given him shelter and protection without which he might have died of hunger. He also told him the story of another young lad whom Fagin had caused to be hanged because he had tried to inform the police.

Little Oliver's blood ran cold, as he listened to the Jew's words and imperfectly understood the dark threats they carried.

The Jew, smiling in an ugly manner, patted Oliver on the head and said that if he kept quiet and did what he was told to do they would be very good friends yet. Then, taking his hat and covering himself with an old over-coat, he went out and locked the room-door behind him.

And so Oliver remained that day, and for the greater part of many days after it, seeing nobody between early morning and midnight, and left during the long hours to his own sad thoughts.

One cold, damp, windy night the old Jew wrapped himself tightly in his overcoat and, pulling the collar up over his ears so as to hide completely the lower part of his face, left his den. He walked along the dark muddy streets until he came to where Bill Sikes lived.

The dog growled as the Jew touched the handle of the room-door; and Bill demanded who was there.

"Only me, Bill; only me, my dear," said the Jew, looking in.

"Come in, then," said Sikes. "Lie down, you stupid brute. Don't you know the devil when he's got a great-coat on? Well!"

"Well, my dear," replied the Jew. "Ah! Nancy." The young lady, who was sitting by the fire, told him to draw up a chair.

"It *is* cold, Nancy dear," said the Jew, as he warmed his skinny hands over the fire. "It seems to go right through one," added the old man, touching his side.

"Give him something to drink, Nancy. Now then, I'm ready; say what you've got to say."

"About the house at Chertsey. When is it to be done, Bill? When is it to be done? Such silver, my dear, such silver!" said the Jew, rubbing his hands.

"Toby Crackit has been hanging about the place for a fortnight, and he can't get one of the servants to help us. The old lady has had them these twenty years, and if you were to give them five hundred pounds, they wouldn't be in it."

"It's a sad thing," said the Jew, "to lose so much when we had set our hearts upon it."

"So it is," said Sikes. "Worse luck!"

After a long silence Sikes suddenly said: "Fagin, will you give me fifty pounds extra, if it's safely done from the outside?"

"Yes," said the Jew.

"Then," said Sikes, "let it come off as soon as you like. Toby and me were over the garden-wall last night, to examine the door and the shutters. The house is barred up at night like a prison; but there's one part we can break through safely."

"Which is that, Bill?" asked the Jew eagerly.

"Never mind which part it is," said Sikes. "You can't do it without me, I know; but it's best to be on the safe side when one deals with you."

C

"As you like, my dear, as you like," replied the Jew. "Is there no help wanted, but yours and Toby's?"

"None," said Sikes, "except a boy; you must find us a little boy."

"Oliver's the boy for you, my dear," replied the Jew in a whisper. "He's been in good training these last few weeks, and it's time he began to work for his bread. Besides, the others are all too big."

"Well, he is just the size I want," said Mr. Sikes.

"And will do everything you want. Bill, my dear," interrupted the Jew, "if you frighten him enough."

"Frighten him!" repeated Sikes. "If he doesn't obey, you won't see him alive again, Fagin. Think of that, before you send him. Mark my words."

"I've thought of it all," said the Jew. "I've had my eye upon him, my dears. Once let him feel that he is one of us; once fill his mind with the idea that he has been a thief, and he's ours! Ours for his life."

"When is it to be done?" asked Nancy.

"I planned with Toby, the night after tomorrow," replied Sikes, "if he heard nothing from me to the contrary."

"Good," said the Jew; "there's no moon."

"No," replied Sikes. "You'd better bring the boy here tomorrow night. I shall leave here an hour after daybreak. All you'll have to do is to hold your tongue and keep the melting pot ready."

After some discussion it was decided that Nancy should go to the Jew's house next evening and bring Oliver away with her, Fagin observing that the boy would be more willing to accompany the girl who had so recently interfered on his behalf, than anybody else.

He looked closely at Nancy before he took his leave. Then he returned to his gloomy house where the Dodger was sitting up, awaiting his return.

Chapter 13

The attempt

When Oliver awoke the next morning the Jew told him that he was to be taken to the house of Bill Sikes that night.

"To . . . to . . . stop there, sir?" asked Oliver, anxiously.

"No, no, my dear. Not to stop there," replied the Jew. "Don't be afraid, Oliver, you shall come back to us. I suppose you want to know what you're going to Bill's for—eh, my dear?"

"Yes, sir, I want to know," replied Oliver.

"Wait till Bill tells you, then," said the Jew.

At night the Jew gave him a candle to burn and a book to read, and told him to wait until they came to fetch him. Then he said to him: "Be careful, Oliver! He is a rough man, and thinks nothing of blood when he is angry. Whatever happens, say nothing, and do what he tells you."

Having given him this warning, the Jew left the house.

Oliver was at a loss as to the real purpose and meaning of Fagin's words. He remained lost in thought for some minutes; and then, with a heavy sigh, he took up the book which the Jew had left him and began to read. The book was all about crime and great criminals. He read of dreadful crimes that made the blood run cold. The terrible descriptions were so real that the pages seemed to turn red with the blood, and the words upon them to be sounded in his ears as if they were whispered by the spirits of the dead.

Seized with great fear, the boy closed the book and pushed it away from him. Then, falling upon his knees, he prayed Heaven to spare him from such deeds and rescue him from his present dangers.

51

He had finished his prayer, but still remained with his head buried in his hands, when he was aroused by a slight noise.

"What's that!" he cried, starting up and catching sight of someone standing by the door. "Who's there?"

"Me. Only me," replied a shaking voice.

Oliver raised the candle above his head, and looked towards the door. It was Nancy.

"Put down the light," said the girl, turning away her head. "It hurts my eyes."

Oliver saw that she was very pale, and gently inquired if she was ill. The girl threw herself into a chair, but made no reply.

"God forgive me!" she cried after a while, "I never thought of this."

She rocked herself to and fro, caught her throat and gasped for breath.

"Nancy!" cried Oliver, "what is it?"

The girl beat her hands upon her knees and trembled with cold. Oliver stirred the fire. Drawing her chair close to it she sat there for a while without speaking; at length she raised her head and looked round.

"I don't know what comes over me sometimes," said she; "it's this damp, dirty room, I think. Now, Nolly, dear, are you ready?"

"Am I to go with you?" asked Oliver.

"Yes. I have come from Bill," replied the girl. "You are to go with me."

"What for?" asked Oliver, drawing back.

"What for?" echoed the girl, raising her eyes and avoiding looking at Oliver. "Oh! for no harm."

"I don't believe it," said Oliver, who had watched her closely.

"Have it your own way," replied the girl, pretending to laugh. "For no good, then."

Oliver could see that he had some power over the girl's better feelings and for an instant thought of appealing to her pity for his helpless state. But then it occurred to him that it was not yet eleven o'clock, and that many people were still in the streets who might help him to get free. He stepped forward and said that he was ready.

The girl eyed him narrowly; she had guessed what had been passing through his mind. She said:

"I have saved you from being ill-treated once, and I will again, and I do now. I have promised that you would be quiet and silent; if you are not, you will only do harm to yourself, and to me, and perhaps be my death. I have borne all this for you already."

She pointed hastily to the blue marks of blows on her neck and arms, and continued:

"Remember this! And don't let me suffer more for you, just now. If I could help you, I would, but I have not the power. They don't mean to harm you; whatever they make you do, is no fault of yours. Hush! Every word from you is a blow for me. Give me your hand. Make haste! Your hand!"

She caught Oliver's hand and, blowing out the candle, drew him after her up the stairs. The door was opened quickly, by someone unseen in the darkness, and was as quickly closed, when they had passed out. A carriage was waiting; the girl pulled Oliver hurriedly in with her, and drew the curtains. The driver needed no directions; he whipped his horse into full speed. The carriage stopped at Bill Sikes's house. In a moment they were inside, and the door was shut.

"This way," said the girl, releasing her hold for the first time. "Bill!"

"Hallo!" replied Sikes, appearing at the head of the stairs with a candle. "Oh! Come on! So you've got the child. Did he come quiet?"

"Like a lamb," said Nancy.

"I'm glad to hear it," said Sikes, looking severely at Oliver, "for his own sake. Come here, my boy, and listen to what I'm going to say."

Mr Sikes, taking Oliver by the shoulder, sat down by the table and stood the boy in front of him.

"Now, first: do you know what this is?" inquired Sikes, taking up a pocket-pistol which lay on the table.

"Yes, sir," said Oliver.

"Well, then, look here," continued Sikes. "This is powder, and this is a bullet." Then, having loaded the pistol, he grasped Oliver's wrist and put the barrel so close to his head that they touched. "If you speak a word," he said, "when you're out with me, except when I speak to you, that bullet will be in your head without notice. So, if you do make up your mind to speak without permission, say your prayers first. And now, Nancy, let's have some supper, and get a short sleep before we start."

It was a cheerless morning when they got into the street; blowing and raining hard; and the clouds looking dull and stormy.

Mr Bill Sikes, holding Oliver firmly by the hand, hurried on through the streets of the great city and along the country roads which at length took their place.

It was quite dark when, through narrow lanes and across muddy fields, they came to a lonely and decayed house. No light could be seen from the windows; the house seemed to be uninhabited. A little pressure on the door from Sikes's hand; it yielded to the pressure and they passed in together.

"Hallo," cried a loud, hoarse voice, as soon as they set foot in the passage.

"Don't make such a noise," said Sikes, bolting the door. "Show a light, Toby."

It was Toby Crackit, a house-breaker.

They entered a low, dark room with a smoky fire, two or three broken chairs, a table and a very old sofa.

"Bill, my boy!" said Mr Crackit, "I'm glad to see you. I was almost afraid you'd given it up; in which case I should have made the attempt without your help. Hallo!"

Uttering this exclamation as his eye rested on Oliver, Mr Toby Crackit demanded who the boy was.

"The boy. Only the boy. Now, if you'll give us something to eat and drink while we're waiting, you'll put some heart in us."

"Here," said Toby, placing some food and a bottle upon the table. "Success to the attempt!" He filled a glass with spirits, and drank off its contents. Mr Sikes did the same.

At half-past one they wrapped their necks and chins in large dark shawls and drew on their great-coats. Toby, opening a cupboard, brought forth a pair of loaded pistols which he pushed into his pockets.

"Now, then," he said, "is everything ready? Nothing forgotten?"

"All right," said Sikes, holding Oliver by the hand. "Take his other hand, Toby."

The two robbers went out with Oliver between them.

It was now very dark. The mist was much heavier than it had been in the early part of the night. They crossed a bridge and soon arrived at the little town of Chertsey. They hurried through the main street, which at that late hour was wholly deserted. Then they turned up a road upon the left hand. After walking about a quarter of a mile they stopped before a house surrounded by a wall, to the top of which Toby Crackit, scarcely pausing to take breath, climbed in a twinkling.

"The boy next," said Toby. "lift him up; I'll catch hold of him."

Before Oliver had time to look round, Sikes had caught him under the arms; and in three or four seconds he and

Toby were lying on the grass on the other side. Sikes followed directly, and they stole cautiously towards the house.

And now, for the first time, Oliver, almost mad with grief and terror, saw that housebreaking and robbery, if not murder, were the objects of their journey. A mist came before his eyes; his face was covered with a cold sweat; his limbs failed him and he sank upon his knees.

"Get up," murmured Sikes, trembling with rage, and drawing the pistol from his pocket. "Get up, or I'll scatter your brains upon the grass."

"Oh! for God's sake let me go!" cried Oliver; "let me run away and die in the fields. I will never come near London; never, never! Oh! pray have mercy on me, and do not make me steal."

Sikes swore a dreadful oath and would have fired the pistol if Toby had not struck it from his hand and, putting his hand upon the boy's mouth, dragged him to the house.

"Hush!" cried Toby; "say another word and I'll knock you down with a crack on the head. That makes no noise, and is quite as certain. Here, Bill, force the shutter open."

After some delay, and some assistance from Toby, the shutter was open. It was a little window about five feet and a half above the ground, at the back of the house. The inmates had probably not thought it worth while to defend it more securely, but it was large enough to admit a boy of Oliver's size.

"Now listen," whispered Sikes, drawing a lantern from his pocket; "I'm going to put you through there. Take this light; go softly up the steps straight before you, and along the little hall, to the street door; unfasten it, and let us in."

Now Toby stood firmly with his head against the wall beneath the window, and his hands upon his knees, so as to make a step of his back. This was no sooner done than

Sikes, mounting upon him, put Oliver gently through the window with his feet first; and without leaving hold of his collar, planted him safely on the inside.

"Take this lantern," said Sikes, looking into the room. "You see the stairs before you."

Oliver, more dead than alive, gasped out, "Yes." Sikes, pointing to the street-door with the pistol-barrel, briefly advised him to take notice that he was within shot all the way; and that if he hesitated, he would fall dead that instant.

"It's done in a minute," said Sikes, in the same low whisper. "Directly I leave go of you, do your work. Listen!"

"What's that?" whispered the other man.

They listened intently.

"Nothing," said Sikes, releasing his hold of Oliver. "Now!"

In the short time he had to collect his senses, the boy had firmly resolved that, whether he died in the attempt or not, he would make one effort to rush upstairs from the hall, and warn the family. Filled with this idea, he advanced at once, but stealthily.

"Come back!" suddenly cried Sikes aloud. "Back! Back!"

Frightened by the sudden noise in the stillness of the night and by a loud cry which followed it, Oliver let his lantern fall, and knew not whether to advance or fly.

The cry was repeated—a light appeared—a vision of two terrified half-dressed men at the top of the stairs swam before his eyes—a flash—a loud noise—a smoke—a crash somewhere.

Sikes had disappeared for an instant; but he was up again, and had him by the collar after the smoke had cleared away. He fired his own pistol after the men, who were already retreating, and dragged the boy up.

"Hold on to me tighter," said Sikes, as he drew him through the window. "Give me a shawl here. They've hit him. Quick! How the boy bleeds!"

Then came the loud ringing of a bell, mixed with the noise of pistols and the shouts of men, and the sensation of being carried over uneven ground at a rapid pace. And then the noises grew confused in the distance; and a cold, deadly feeling crept over the boy's heart; and he saw and heard no more.

Chapter 14

Mr Giles catches a thief!

"Wolves tear your throats!" muttered Sikes, grinding his teeth and resting the body of the wounded boy in a dry ditch. "I wish I was among some of you; you'd howl the hoarser for it."

At this moment the noise grew louder. The pursuers were already climbing the gate of the field in which he stood, and a couple of dogs were paces in advance of them.

"It's all up, Bill!" cried Toby; "leave the boy and show them your heels." With this parting advice, Mr Crackit turned and ran at full speed. Sikes took one look around, threw a shawl over Oliver, and running along the hedge for some distance, he was over it at one jump and was gone.

The three pursuers called back their dogs and stopped to take counsel together.

"My advice is," said the fattest man of the party, "that we immediately go home again."

"I agree with you, Mr Giles," said a shorter man called Mr Brittles, who was very pale and frightened. In fact all three men were afraid, although they were ashamed to admit it at first.

Mr Giles was head servant to the old lady of the house where the robbery had been attempted. Brittles was a lad of all work who, having entered her service as a mere child, was treated as a young boy still, though he was something past thirty. The third man was a travelling tinker who had joined in the pursuit together with his two dogs.

Encouraging each other with conversation and keeping very close together, the three men made the best of their way home at a good pace.

The air grew colder, as day came slowly on; and the mist rolled along the ground like a thick cloud of smoke. Still, Oliver lay motionless and insensible in the place where Sikes had left him.

Morning drew on fast. The air became more sharp and piercing. The rain came down, thick and fast, but Oliver felt it not, as it beat against him; for he still lay stretched, helpless and unconscious, on his bed of clay.

At length the boy awoke, uttering a low cry of pain. His left arm, bandaged in a shawl, hung heavy and useless at his side. He was so weak that he could scarcely raise himself into a sitting position, but he managed at last to get up and walk unsteadily, he knew not where. He staggered on until he reached a road and, looking about, he saw a house at no great distance, towards which he directed his steps, hoping to get some assistance there. He walked across the lawn, climbed the steps, knocked faintly at the door, and then, his whole strength failing him, he sank down on the door-step.

It happened about this time that Mr Giles, Brittles and the tinker were having tea in the kitchen. Mr Giles was giving his hearers (including the cook and housemaid) a detailed account of the robbery, to which they listened with breathless interest.

"It was about half-past two," said Mr Giles, "when I woke up and, turning round, I fancied I heard a noise."

At this point of the story, the cook turned pale and asked the housemaid to shut the door; the housemaid asked Brittles, and Brittles asked the tinker, who pretended not to hear.

". . . heard a noise," continued Mr Giles. "I said to myself, at first, This is only your fancy, Giles, and was preparing to fall asleep again when I heard the noise distinctly, once more."

"Good Lord!" exclaimed the cook and housemaid at the same time, and drew their chairs closer together.

"I heard it now, quite distinctly," resumed Mr Giles. "Somebody, I said to myself, is forcing a door or a window; what's to be done? I'll call up that poor lad, Brittles, and save him from being murdered in his bed, or having his throat cut."

Here all eyes were turned upon Brittles, who stared at the speaker, with his mouth wide open, and his face a perfect expression of horror.

"I tossed off the bed clothes," said Giles, "got softly out of bed, seized a loaded pistol and walked on tiptoe to his room. 'Brittles,' I said, when I had woke him, 'don't be frightened!'"

"So you did," observed Brittles, in a low voice.

"'We're dead men, I think, Brittles,' I said," continued Giles; "'but don't be frightened.'"

"*Was* he frightened?" asked the cook.

"Not a bit of it," replied Mr Giles. "He was as firm—ah! pretty near as firm as I was."

"I should have died at once, I'm sure, if it had been me," observed the housemaid.

"You're a woman," said Brittles.

"Brittles is right," said Mr Giles, nodding his head approvingly; "from a woman, nothing else was to be expected. We, being men, took a dark lantern and groped our way downstairs in the pitch dark—as it might be so."

Mr Giles had risen from his seat, and taken two steps with his eyes shut, to accompany his description with action, when he started violently, together with the rest of the company, and hurried back to his chair. The cook and housemaid screamed.

"It was a knock," said Mr Giles, pretending to be perfectly calm. "Open the door, somebody."

Nobody moved.

"It seems a strange sort of thing, a knock coming at such a time in the morning," said Mr Giles, looking at the pale faces round him, and looking pale himself; "but the door must be opened. Do you hear, somebody?"

Mr Giles, as he spoke, looked at Brittles, but that young man, being naturally modest, probably considered himself nobody, and so he gave no reply. Mr Giles looked appealingly at the tinker, but he had suddenly fallen asleep. The women were out of the question.

"If Brittles would rather open the door in the presence of witnesses," said Mr Giles, after a short silence, "I am ready to make one."

"So am I," said the tinker, waking up as suddenly as he had fallen asleep.

Brittles consented to open the door on these terms, and they took their way upstairs, with the dogs in front. The two women, who were afraid to stay below, brought up the rear. By the advice of Mr Giles, they all talked very loud, to warn any one outside that they were strong in numbers. Mr Giles also made them pinch the dogs' tails in the hall, to make them bark savagely.

These precautions having been taken, Mr Giles gave the word of command to open the door. Brittles obeyed; the group, looking fearfully over each other's shoulders, saw no more formidable object than poor little Oliver Twist, speechless and fatigued, who raised his heavy eyes, and silently begged their pity.

"A boy!" exclaimed Mr Giles, bravely pushing the tinker into the background, and dragging Oliver into the hall. Then he called aloud, in a state of great excitement: "Here he is! Here's one of the thieves, ma'am! here's a thief, miss! Wounded, miss! I shot him, miss!"

The two women-servants ran upstairs to carry the news that Mr Giles had captured a robber; and the tinker busied himself in trying to restore Oliver, lest he should die before he could be hanged. In the midst of all this noise there was heard a sweet female voice.

"Giles!" whispered the voice from the head of the stairs.

"I'm here, miss," replied Mr Giles. "Don't be frightened, miss, I'm not much injured. He didn't struggle very hard, miss."

"Hush!" replied the young lady, "you frighten my aunt as much as the thieves did. Is the poor creature much hurt?"

"He's badly wounded, miss," replied Giles.

"He looks as if he was dying, miss," called out Brittles, loudly. "Wouldn't you like to come and look at him, miss, in case he dies?"

"Hush!" said the lady again. "Wait quietly only an instant, while I speak to aunt."

The speaker walked softly away and presently returned and ordered that the wounded person was to be carried carefully upstairs to Mr Giles's room, and that Brittles was to go at once to Chertsey and fetch a policeman and a doctor.

"But won't you take one look at him, first, miss?" asked Mr Giles, with as much pride as if Oliver were some rare bird he had shot down. "Not one little look, miss?"

"Not now, Giles," replied the young lady. "Poor fellow! Oh! treat him kindly, Giles, for my sake!"

The old servant looked up at the young lady, as she turned away, with a glance as proud and admiring as if she had been his own child. Then, bending over Oliver, he helped to carry him upstairs with the care and gentleness of a woman.

Fagin the Jew, Charlie Bates and the Dodger were playing cards when the Dodger cried: "Listen! I heard the bell!" and, catching up the light, he crept softly upstairs.

The bell was rung again, with some impatience, while the card party were in darkness. After a short pause, the Dodger reappeared, and whispered something to Fagin.

"What!" cried the Jew, "alone?"

The Dodger nodded in the affirmative and admitted Toby Crackit.

"How are you, Faguey?" said Toby and then, drawing a chair to the fire, he sat down. "Don't look at me in that way, man. All in good time; I can't talk about business till I've eaten and drunk, for I haven't had a good meal these three days."

The Jew motioned to the Dodger to place what food there was upon the table, and seating himself opposite the housebreaker, waited to listen to what he had to say.

Toby was in no hurry to open the conversation. At first the Jew watched his face patiently, as if to gain from its expression some clue to the information he brought, but in vain. Toby continued to eat with the utmost indifference until he could eat no more; then, ordering Charlie Bates and the Dodger out, he closed the door, mixed a glass of spirits and water and said:

"First of all, Faguey, how's Bill?"

"What!" screamed the Jew, starting from his seat.

"Why, you don't mean to say——" began Toby, turning pale.

"Mean?" cried the Jew, stamping furiously on the ground. "Where are they? Sikes and the boy! Where are they? Where have they been? Where are they hiding? Why have they not been here?"

"The attempt failed," said Toby faintly.

"I know it," replied the Jew, taking a newspaper out of his pocket and pointing to it. "What more?"

"They fired and hit the boy. We cut across the fields at the back, with him between us. They gave chase, damn them. The whole countryside was awake, and the dogs upon us."

"The boy!"

"Bill had him on his back, and fled like the wind. We stopped to take him between us; his head hung down, and he was cold. They were close upon our heels; every man for himself, and each from the gallows! We parted company, and left the boy lying in a ditch, alive or dead I don't know."

The Jew stopped to hear no more; but uttering a loud scream, and tearing his hair with his hands, he rushed from the room and from the house.

Chapter 15

A mysterious character appears upon the scene

Fagin had gained the street corner before he began to recover from the effect of Toby Crackit's information. Avoiding, as much as possible, all the main streets, he at length came to a public house called The Three Cripples, which was the favourite haunt of thieves and criminals.

He walked straight upstairs, and, opening the door of a room, looked anxiously about, shading his eyes with his hand, as if in search of some particular person. The room was lit by two gas-lights, the glare of which was prevented by the barred shutters and closely-drawn curtains from being visible outside. The place was so full of tobacco smoke that at first it was scarcely possible to see anything more. Gradually, however, as the eye grew more accustomed to the scene, the spectator became aware of the presence of a numerous company, male and female, crowded round a long table, drinking and singing noisily.

Fagin looked eagerly from face to face, but apparently without meeting that of which he was in search. At last, catching the eye of the landlord, he made a slight signal to him and left the room.

"What can I do for you, Mr Fagin?" inquired the man, as he followed him out to the landing. "Won't you join us? They'll be delighted, every one of them."

The Jew shook his head impatiently, and said in a whisper. "Is *he* here?"

"Monks, do you mean?" inquired the landlord, hesitating.

"Hush!" said the Jew. "Yes."

"No," said the man, "but I'm expecting him. If you'll wait ten minutes, he'll be——"

"No, no," said the Jew; "tell him I came here to see him; and that he must come to me tonight."

So saying the Jew left the place and turned his face homeward. It was within an hour of midnight; the weather was piercing cold and a sharp wind was blowing. He had reached the corner of his own street when a dark figure emerged from the darkness and, crossing the road, came up to him unnoticed.

65

"Fagin!" whispered a voice close to his ear.

"Ah!" said the Jew, turning quickly round, "is that——"

"Yes!" interrupted the stranger. "I have been lingering here these two hours. Where the devil have you been?"

"Looking for you at The Three Cripples. On your business all night."

"Oh, of course!" said the stranger, with a sneer. "Well; and what's come of it?"

"Nothing good," said the Jew.

They went inside together, and talked for some time in whispers. Then Monks, for this was the stranger's name, said, raising his voice a little:

"I tell you again, it was badly planned. Why not have kept him here among the rest, and made a pickpocket of him at once?"

"Only hear him!" exclaimed the Jew, shrugging his shoulders.

"Why, do you mean to say you couldn't have done it, if you had chosen?" demanded Monks, sternly. "Haven't you done it, with other boys, scores of times? If you had had more patience, couldn't you have got him arrested and sent safely out of the kingdom, perhaps for life?"

"Whose turn would that have served, my dear?" inquired the Jew humbly.

"Mine," replied Monks.

"But not mine," replied the Jew. "He might have become of use to me. When there are two parties to a bargain, it is only reasonable that the interests of both should be consulted. I saw it was not easy to train him to the business; he was not like other boys in the same circumstances."

"Curse him, no," muttered the man, "or he would have been a thief long ago."

"I had no hold upon him to make him worse," pursued the Jew. "I had nothing to frighten him with; which we must always have in the beginning, or we labour in vain. What could I do? Send him out with the Dodger and Charlie? We had enough of that at first, my dear; I trembled for us all."

"That was not my doing," observed Monks.

"No, no, my dear," replied the Jew. "And I don't quarrel with it now; because if it had never happened you might never have seen the boy you were looking for. Well! I got him back for you by means of the girl; and then *she* begins to favour him."

"Kill the girl," said Monks, impatiently.

"Why, we can't afford to do that just now, my dear," replied the Jew, smiling; "and, besides, that sort of thing is not in our way; or, one of these days, I might be glad to have done it. I know what these girls are, Monks. As soon as the boy begins to harden, she'll care no more for him than for a block of wood. You want him made a thief. If he is alive, I can make him one but if the worst comes to the worst, and he is dead——"

"It's no fault of mine if he is!" interrupted the other man, with a look of terror, and grasping the Jew's arm with trembling hands. "Mind that, Fagin! I had no hand in it. Anything but his death, I told you from the first. I won't shed blood; it's always found out, and haunts a man besides. If they shot him dead, I was not the cause; do you hear me? Oh! what's that?"

"What?" cried the Jew, grasping the coward with both arms as he jumped to his feet. "Where?"

"There!" replied the man, glaring at the opposite wall. "The shadow! I saw the shadow of a woman, in a cloak and bonnet, pass along the wall like a breath!"

The Jew released his hold and they both rushed out of the room. There was nothing but the empty staircase. They listened intently: a deep silence reigned throughout the house.

"It's your fancy," said the Jew, turning to his companion.

"I'll swear I saw it," replied Monks trembling. "It was bending forward when I saw it first; and, when I spoke, it darted away."

The Jew looked contemptuously at the pale face of his companion, and told him he could accompany him upstairs, if he wished. They looked into the rooms; they were cold, bare and empty. They descended into the passage, and from there into the cellars below; all was empty and still as death.

Chapter 16

The kind-hearted Dr Losberne

In a handsome, comfortably furnished room there sat two ladies at a breakfast table. Mr Giles, dressed neatly in the black suit of a butler, was waiting upon them. Of the two ladies one was advanced in years, but she sat upright in her chair, with her hands folded on the table before her. Her eyes were attentively fixed upon her young companion.

The young lady was in the lovely bloom and springtime of womanhood. She was not past seventeen; she had such a slight and delicate form, she was so mild and gentle, so pure and beautiful, that earth seemed not her element, nor its rough creatures her fit companions.

"And Brittles has been gone more than an hour, has he?" asked the old lady, after a pause.

"An hour and twelve minutes, ma'am," replied Mr Giles, consulting a silver watch which he drew forth with a black ribbon. At this moment a carriage drove up to the garden gate, out of which there jumped a fat gentleman who ran straight up to the door and, bursting into the room, nearly overturned Mr Giles and the breakfast table together.

"I never heard of such a thing!" exclaimed the fat gentleman. "My dear Mrs Maylie—bless my soul—in the silence of the night, too—I *never* heard of such a thing!"

With these exclamations, the fat gentleman shook hands with both ladies, and, drawing up a chair, inquired how they found themselves.

"Why didn't you send? Bless me, my assistant should have come in a minute; and so would I. Dear, dear! So unexpected! In the silence of night, too!"

The doctor seemed especially troubled by the fact that the robbery had been unexpected, and attempted in the night-time; as if it were the custom of robbers to do their business at noon, and to make an appointment, by post, a day or two in advance.

"And you, Miss Rose," said the doctor, turning to the young lady, "I——"

"Oh! very much so, indeed," said Rose, interrupting; "but there is a poor creature upstairs, whom aunt wishes you to see."

"Ah! to be sure," replied the doctor, "so there is." Then, turning to Giles, he asked him to show him the way.

Talking all the way, he followed Mr Giles upstairs, and while he is going upstairs the reader may be informed that the doctor was called Mr Losberne, and that he was as kind and hearty as any doctor living.

The doctor remained a long time upstairs. A large box was fetched out of the carriage, and a bedroom bell was rung often. At length he returned to the ladies, looking very mysterious.

"This is a very extraordinary thing, Mrs Maylie," said the doctor.

"He is not in danger, I hope?" said the old lady.

"I don't think he is," replied the doctor. "Have you seen the thief?"

"No," replied the old lady.

"Nor heard anything about him?"

"No."

"I beg your pardon, ma'am," interrupted Mr Giles; "but I was going to tell you about him when Dr Losberne came in."

The fact was that Mr Giles had received such praise of his bravery that he could not help postponing the explanation for a few happy moments.

"Rose wished to see the man," said Mrs Maylie, "but I wouldn't hear of it."

"There is nothing very alarming in his appearance," replied the doctor. "Have you any objection to seeing him in my presence?"

"If it is necessary," replied the old lady, "certainly not."

"I think it is necessary," said the doctor; "at all events, I am quite sure you would deeply regret it if you did not. He is perfectly quiet and comfortable now. I would like you both to come and see him."

He led the way upstairs to Giles's room where, instead of the evil-faced criminal they expected to see, there lay a child upon the bed; a mere child, worn with pain and fatigue, and sunk into a deep sleep. His bandaged arm was crossed upon his breast, and his head leaned upon the other arm.

The honest doctor watched the patient in silence while the younger lady seated herself in a chair by the bedside. As she bent over the child her tears fell upon his forehead. The boy stirred, and smiled in his sleep, as if these marks of pity had awakened some pleasant dream of love and affection he had never known.

70

"What can this mean?" exclaimed the elder lady. "This poor child can never have been the pupil of robbers!"

"My dear lady," said the doctor, sadly shaking his head, "crime, like death, is not confined to the old and ugly alone. The youngest and fairest are too often its chosen victims."

"But can you really believe that this delicate boy has been the voluntary partner of criminals?" said Rose.

The doctor shook his head, as if to say that he feared it was very possible; and, observing that they might disturb the patient, led the way into another room.

"But even if he has been wicked," pursued Rose, "think how young he is, think that he may never have known a mother's love, or the comfort of a home; that ill-treatment and blows, or the want of bread, may have driven him into the company of men who have forced him to lead a life of crime. Aunt, dear aunt, for mercy's sake, think of this, before you let them drag this sick child to a prison. Oh! as you love me, who might have been helpless and unprotected but for your goodness and affection, have pity upon him before it is too late!"

"My dear love," said the elder lady, "do you think I would harm a hair of his head? No, surely. My days are drawing to their close; and may mercy be shown to me as I show it to others! What can I do to save him, sir?"

"Let me think, ma'am," said the doctor; "let me think."

Dr Losberne thrust his hands into his pockets, and took several turns up and down the room; often stopping and balancing himself on his toes, and frowning frightfully. After various exclamations of "I've got it now," and "no, I haven't," he at length came to a standstill.

Hour after hour passed on, and still Oliver slept heavily. It was evening, indeed, before the kind-hearted doctor brought them the news that the boy was sufficiently restored to be spoken to.

Oliver told them all his simple history, and was often compelled to stop by pain or weakness. It was a solemn thing to hear, in the darkened room, the feeble voice of the sick child narrating the many evils and misfortunes which hard men had brought upon him. But his pillow was smoothed by gentle hands that night, and beauty and virtue watched him as he slept.

Dr Losberne went down to the kitchen to talk to Mr Giles.

"How is the patient tonight, sir?" asked Giles.

"So-so," returned the doctor. "I am afraid you have got yourself into trouble there, Mr Giles."

"I hope you don't mean to say, sir," said Mr Giles, trembling, "that he's going to die. If I thought it, I should never be happy again."

"That's not the point," said the doctor mysteriously. "The point is this: are you ready to swear, you and Brittles here, that that boy upstairs is the boy that was put through the little window last night? Out with it! Come! We are prepared for you!"

The doctor made this demand in such a dreadful tone of pretended anger that Giles and Brittles stared at each other in confusion.

"Here's a house broken into," said the doctor, "and a couple of men catch one moment's glimpse of a boy, in the midst of gunpowder-smoke, and in all the confusion of alarm and darkness. Here's a boy who comes to that same house, next morning, and because he happens to have his arm tied up, these men lay violent hands upon him—by doing which they put his life in great danger—and swear he is the thief. Now, the question is, whether these men are justified in so doing. I ask you again, Giles and Brittles, are you, on your solemn oaths, able to identify that boy?"

Brittles looked doubtfully at Mr Giles; Mr Giles looked

72

doubtfully at Brittles; the two women and the tinker leaned forward to listen; when a ring was heard at the gate, and at the same moment the sound of wheels. It was the police officers who had been sent for.

Dr Losberne led them upstairs to Oliver's bedroom. Oliver had been dozing, but he was still feverish. Being assisted by the doctor, he managed to sit up in bed for a minute or so, and looked at the strangers without at all understanding what was going on.

"This," said Dr Losberne, "is the lad who, being accidentally wounded by a spring-gun, comes to the house for assistance this morning, and is immediately arrested and ill-treated by that gentleman with the candle in his hand."

Mr Giles was in a miserable condition of fear and amazement. The police officers questioned him; all he could say at first was that he *thought* the boy was the housebreaker's boy; then, on being further questioned, he said he didn't know what to think; he couldn't swear to him; at last he said that he was almost certain it wasn't the same boy.

In short, after some more examination, and a great deal more conversation, the police officers were convinced that Giles had made a stupid mistake and that Oliver had nothing to do with the housebreakers. Both policemen returned to town, and Oliver was left to the loving care of Mrs Maylie, Rose and the kind-hearted Dr Losberne.

Chapter 17

Oliver's life with the Maylies

Oliver's sufferings were neither slight nor few. In addition to the pain of a broken limb, his exposure to the wet and cold had brought on fever which hung about him for many weeks, and reduced him sadly. But at length he began, by slow degrees, to get better, and was able to say, in a few tearful words, how deeply he felt the goodness of the two sweet ladies, and how sincerely he hoped that when he grew strong and well again he could do something to show his gratitude.

"Poor fellow!" said Rose, when Oliver had been one day feebly trying to utter the words of thankfulness that rose to his pale lips; "you shall have many opportunities of serving us, if you will. We are going into the country, and my aunt intends that you shall accompany us. The quiet place, the pure air, and all the pleasures and beauties of spring, will restore you in a few days. We will employ you in a hundred ways, when you can bear the trouble."

"The trouble!" cried Oliver. "Oh! dear lady, if I could but work for you!"

"You shall," said Rose.

A fortnight later, when the fine warm weather had fairly begun, and every tree and flower was putting forth its young leaves and rich blossoms, they made preparations for leaving the house at Chertsey for some months. Leaving Giles and another servant in charge of the house, they departed to a cottage at some distance in the country, and took Oliver with them.

It was a lovely spot to which they had gone. Oliver, whose days had been spent in the midst of noise and quarrelling, seemed to enter on a new existence there. The days were peaceful and calm; the nights brought with them neither fear nor care; no suffering in a wretched prison or associating with wretched men; nothing but pleasant and happy thoughts. Every morning he went to an old gentleman who lived near the little village church, who taught him to read better, and to write. Then he would walk with Mrs Maylie and Rose, and hear them talk of books; or perhaps sit near them, in some shady place, and listen while the young lady read. Then he had his own lesson to prepare for the next day. In the evening there were more walks, and at night the young lady would sit down to the piano and play some pleasant tune, or sing in a low gentle voice, some old song which it pleased her aunt to hear.

So three months passed away; three months of perfect happiness. With the purest and most amiable generosity on one side, and the warmest gratitude on the other, it is no wonder that, by the end of that short time, Oliver Twist had become a strongly-attached and dearly-beloved member of the small family.

Chapter 18

The mysterious character reappears

Mr Bumble, who was now a married man, and master of the workhouse, feeling miserable one day after a little family quarrel with Mrs Bumble, left the workhouse and walked about the streets. Feeling thirsty, he paused before a public-house whose parlour, as he gathered from a hasty peep over the blinds, was deserted, except by one solitary customer. It began to rain heavily at the moment. This determined him; he stepped in and, ordering something to drink as he passed the bar, entered the room into which he had looked from the street.

The man who was seated there was tall and dark, and wore a large cloak. He had the air of a stranger, and seemed by the dustiness of his clothes to have travelled some distance. He eyed Bumble sideways as he entered, but scarcely answered his greeting. Mr Bumble drank his gin-and-water in silence, and read the paper with an air of importance.

It happened, however, as will happen very often, when men fall into company under such circumstances, that Mr Bumble felt, every now and then, a strong desire to steal a look at the stranger. Whenever he did so he found that the stranger was at the same moment stealing a look at him.

When their eyes had met several times in this way the stranger said in a harsh, deep voice:

"Were you looking for me when you looked in at the window?"

"Not that I am aware of, unless you're Mr ——" Here Mr Bumble stopped short, for he was curious to know the stranger's name, and thought that he might supply the blank.

"I see you were not," said the stranger, "or you would have known my name. But I know you pretty well. What are you now?"

"Master of the workhouse," answered Mr Bumble, slowly and impressively.

"You have the same eye to your interest that you always had, I doubt not?" resumed the stranger, looking keenly into Mr Bumble's eyes, as he raised them in astonishment at the question.

"I suppose a married man," replied Mr Bumble, "has no more objection to earning an honest penny than a single man. Workhouse masters are not so well paid that they can afford to refuse any little extra money when it comes to them in the proper manner."

The stranger smiled, and nodded his head, as much as to say, he had not mistaken his man; then he rang the bell.

"Fill this glass again," he said, handing Mr Bumble's empty glass to the landlord. "Let it be strong and hot. You like it so, I suppose?"

"Not too strong," replied Mr Bumble, with a delicate cough.

The host smiled, disappeared, and shortly afterwards returned with a steaming glass, of which the first mouthful brought tears into Mr Bumble's eyes.

"Now listen to me," said the stranger, after closing the door and window. "I came down to this place today to find you out. I want some information from you. I don't ask you to give it for nothing, slight as it is."

As he spoke he pushed a couple of gold pounds across the table to his companion. When Mr Bumble had carefully examined the coins, to see that they were real gold, and put them in his pocket, the stranger went on:

"Carry your memory back—let me see—twelve years, last winter."

"It's a long time," said Mr Bumble. "Very good. I've done it."

"The scene, the workhouse."

"Good!"

"And the time, night."

"Yes."

"And the place, the miserable room where wretched women gave birth to children for the parish to rear and hid their shame in the grave! A boy was born there."

"Many boys," observed Mr. Bumble.

"I speak of one; a gentle-looking, pale-faced boy, who was apprenticed down here to a coffin-maker—I wish he

77

had made his coffin, and screwed his body in it—and who afterwards ran away to London."

"Why, you mean Oliver! Young Twist!" said Mr Bumble; "I remember him, of course. There wasn't a more obstinate young rascal——"

"It's not of him I want to hear," said the stranger, "it's of a woman, the old woman who nursed his mother. Where is she?"

"She died last winter," answered Mr. Bumble.

The man looked fixedly at him when he had given this information. For some time, he appeared doubtful whether he ought to be relieved or disappointed by the information; but at length he observed that it was no great matter, and rose to depart.

But Mr Bumble saw at once that an opportunity was opened for him to make some money. He remembered that his wife, who had been a nurse in the workhouse before he married her, was in possession of a secret related to that old woman. He informed the stranger that one woman had been alone with the old nurse shortly before she died; and that she could throw some light on the subject of his inquiry.

"How can I find her?" said the stranger, thrown off his guard, and plainly showing that this information aroused his fears again.

"Only through me," replied Mr Bumble.

"When?" cried the stranger, hastily.

"Tomorrow," replied Mr Bumble.

"At nine in the evening," said the stranger, producing a piece of paper, and writing down upon it an obscure address by the waterside. "At nine in the evening bring her to me there. I needn't tell you to be secret. It's your interest."

With these words he got up, paid for the drinks and departed.

On looking at the address Mr Bumble observed that it

contained no name. He ran after the stranger and said:
"What name am I to ask for?"

"Monks!" replied the man, and walked hastily away.

Chapter 19

A meeting at night

It was a dull, rainy summer evening when Mr and Mrs
Bumble, turning out of the main street of the town, directed
their course towards a group of ruined houses, about a
mile and a half away from it, built on a low unhealthy
swamp bordering upon the river.

In the heart of this group of buildings, and bordering the
river, stood a larger building, formerly used as a factory of
some kind, but it had long since gone to ruin. It was before
this decayed building that Mr and Mrs Bumble stopped.

"The place should be somewhere here," said Bumble,
consulting a scrap of paper he held in his hand.

"Hallo there!" cried a voice from above. "Stand still a
minute. I'll be with you directly."

Presently a small door opened and Monks signalled them
inwards.

"Come in!" he cried impatiently, stamping his foot
upon the ground. "Don't keep me here!"

The woman, who had hesitated at first, walked boldly in,
followed, rather unwillingly, by Mr Bumble. Monks led
the way up a ladder to another floor above and hastily
closed the door of the room in which they were. Then he
lowered a lantern which hung at the end of a rope and
which cast a dim light upon an old table and three chairs
that were placed beneath it.

"Now," said Monks, when they had all three seated themselves, "the sooner we come to our business the better for all. The woman knows what it is, does she?"

Mrs Bumble said that she was perfectly acquainted with it.

"He is right in saying that you were with this old nurse the night she died, and that she told you something——"

"About the mother of the boy you named," replied Mrs Bumble, interrupting him. "Yes."

"The first question is, of what nature was her information?" said Monks.

"That's the second," observed the woman with much determination. "The first is, what may the information be worth?"

"Who the devil can tell that, without knowing of what kind it is?" asked Monks.

"Nobody better than you, I am sure," answered Mrs Bumble.

"How much do you want?" asked Monks sternly.

"What's it worth to you?" asked the woman coolly.

"It may be nothing; it may be twenty pounds," replied Monks. "Speak out, and let me know which."

"Add five pounds to the sum you have named, give me five-and-twenty pounds in gold," said the woman, "and I'll tell you all I know. Not before."

"What if I pay it for nothing?" asked Monks, hesitating.

"You can easily take it away again," replied the woman. "I am but a woman, alone here and unprotected."

"Not alone, my dear, nor unprotected either," said Mr Bumble, in a voice trembling with fear. "I am here, my dear."

"You are a fool," said Mrs Bumble in reply, "and had better hold your tongue."

Mr Monks thrust his hand into a side-pocket and, producing a canvas bag, counted out twenty-five gold pounds on the table and pushed them over to the woman.

"Now," he said, "gather them up and let's hear your story."

"When this woman, the woman we called Old Sally, died," Mrs Bumble began, "she and I were alone, I stood beside the body when death came over it. She spoke of a young woman who had brought a child into the world some years before. The child was the one you named to him last night," said the woman, nodding carelessly towards her husband; "the mother was robbed by the nurse."

"In life?" asked Monks.

"In death," replied Mrs Bumble. "She stole from the dead body something which the dead mother had prayed her, with her last breath, to keep for the child's sake."

"She sold it?" cried Monks desperately; "did she sell it? Where? When? To whom? How long ago?"

"As she told me, with great difficulty, that she had done this," said the woman, "she fell back and died."

"Without saying more?" cried Monks, furiously. "It's a lie! I'll not be played with. She said more. I'll tear the life out of you both, but I'll know what it was."

"She didn't utter another word," said the woman, to all appearance unmoved by the strange man's violence; "but she clutched my gown violently with one hand, which was partly closed; and when I saw that she was dead and removed the hand by force, I found it held a bit of jewellery."

"Where is it now?" asked Monks quickly.

"There," replied the woman, and she threw upon the table a small leather bag which Monks tore open with trembling hands. It contained a little gold locket, in which were two locks of hair, and a plain gold wedding ring.

"And is this all?" said Monks, after carefully examining the contents of the little packet.

"All," replied the woman. "Is that what you expected to get from me?"

"It is," replied Monks.

"What do you propose to do with it? Can it be used against me?"

"Never," replied Monks; "nor against me either. See here! But don't move a step forward, or your life is not worth a straw."

With these words he suddenly pushed the table aside, and, pulling an iron ring in the boards of the floor, threw back a large trap-door which opened at Mr Bumble's feet, and caused that gentleman to retire several steps backward with great haste.

"Look down," said Monks, lowering the lantern through the opening. "Don't fear me. I could have let you down, quietly enough, when you were seated over it, if that had been my intention."

Thus encouraged, Mr and Mrs Bumble drew near to the edge of the opening; the muddy water, swollen by the heavy rain, was rushing rapidly on below.

Monks drew the little packet from his breast, where he had hurriedly thrust it, and, tying it to a piece of lead, dropped it into the stream. It fell straight into the water and was gone.

The three looking into each other's faces seemed to breathe more freely.

"There!" said Monks, closing the trap-door. "Light your lantern, and get away from here as fast as you can."

Mr Bumble lighted his lantern and descended the ladder in silence, followed by his wife, and Monks brought up the rear.

They crossed the lower room slowly, and with caution,

for Monks started at every shadow; and Mr Bumble, holding his lantern a foot above the ground, looked nervously about him for hidden trap-doors. The gate at which they had entered was softly unfastened and opened by Monks, and the married couple emerged into the wet and darkness outside.

Chapter 20

Bill Sikes is ill

On the next evening Bill Sikes, awakening from a short sleep, angrily enquired what time of night it was.

"Not long gone seven," said Nancy. "How do you feel tonight, Bill?"

"As weak as water," replied Mr Sikes. "Here, lend me a hand and help me to get off this bed."

Illness had not improved Mr Sikes's temper, for, as the girl raised him up and led him to a chair, he cursed her awkwardness and struck her.

The room in which they were was not the one they had lived in before the attempted robbery at Chertsey, although it was in the same part of the town. It was a small, poorly furnished room, overlooking a narrow, dirty lane. It was evident that Mr Sikes and Nancy now lived in a state of extreme poverty.

"Don't be too hard upon me tonight, Bill," said the girl putting her hand upon his shoulder.

"Why not?" cried Sikes.

"Such a number of nights," said the girl, with a touch of womanly tenderness, "I have been nursing and caring for you, as if you had been a child. And this is the first night that I've seen you better and like yourself. You wouldn't have treated me as you did just now if you'd thought of that, would you? Come, come; say you wouldn't."

"Well, then," replied Mr Sikes, "I wouldn't. But don't stand crying there. You won't affect me with your woman's nonsense."

At that moment Fagin appeared at the door, followed by the Artful Dodger and Charlie Bates.

"Why, what evil wind has blown you here?" said Mr Sikes to Fagin.

"Ah!" said Fagin, rubbing his hands with great satisfaction. "You're better, Bill, I can see."

"Better!" exclaimed Mr Sikes. "I might have been dead twenty times over before you'd have done anything to help me. What do you mean by leaving a man in this state three weeks and more, you false-hearted villain? If it hadn't been for the girl I might have died."

"There now, Bill," said Fagin, eagerly catching at the word. "If it hadn't been for the girl! Who but poor old Fagin was the means of your having such a useful girl about you?"

"He says true enough there!" said Nancy.

"Oh, well," said Mr Sikes to the Jew, "but I must have some money from you tonight."

"I haven't a piece of coin about me," replied the Jew.

"But you've got lots at home," said Sikes, "and I must have some from there."

"Lots!" cried Fagin, holding up his hands. "I haven't so much as would——"

"I don't know how much you've got," said Sikes; "but I must have some tonight."

"Well, well," said Fagin, with a sigh. "I'll send the Artful presently."

"You won't do anything of the kind," replied Mr Sikes.

"Nancy shall go and get it, to make all sure; and I'll lie down and have a short sleep while she's gone."

The Jew then took leave of Sikes and returned home, accompanied by Nancy and the boys.

In due course they arrived at Fagin's house. The Jew sent the boys away from the room and then said to Nancy: "I'll go and get you that money, Nancy. This is only the key of a little cupboard where I keep a few odd things the boys get, my dear. I never lock up my money, for I've got none to lock up, my dear. It's a poor trade, Nancy; and no thanks; but I'm fond of seeing the young people about me; and I bear it all, I bear it all. Hush!" he said hastily, concealing the key in his breast, "who's that? Listen!"

The visitor, coming hastily into the room, was close upon the girl before he observed her.

It was Monks.

"Only one of my young people," said Fagin, observing that Monks drew back, on seeing a stranger. Then pointing upward, he took Monks out of the room.

Before the sound of their footsteps had ceased to echo through the house the girl had slipped off her shoes; then she softly ascended the stairs and was lost in the gloom above.

The room remained deserted for a quarter of an hour or more; the girl glided back softly, and immediately afterwards the two men were heard descending. Monks went at once into the street; and Fagin crawled upstairs again for the money. When he returned, the girl was preparing to go.

"Why, Nance," exclaimed the Jew, starting back as he put down the candle, "how pale you are!"

With a sigh for every piece of money, Fagin counted the amount into her hand, and they parted without more conversation. When the girl got into the open street, she sat down upon a doorstep; and seemed, for a few moments, wholly amazed and unable to pursue her way. Suddenly she arose and hurrying on she soon reached the dwelling where she had left the housebreaker.

Sikes did not observe the agitated condition in which she was. He merely inquired if she had brought the money, and receiving a reply in the affirmative he uttered a growl of satisfaction and resumed the sleep which her arrival had interrupted.

Chapter 21

Nancy pays a secret visit

Sikes was too much occupied, the next day, eating and drinking with the money the girl had brought, to notice anything unusual in her behaviour. But as that day closed in, the girl's excitement increased and when night came on and she sat by, watching until the housebreaker should drink himself asleep, there was an unusual paleness in her cheek, and a fire in her eye, that even Sikes observed with astonishment.

"Why?" said the man, raising himself on his hands as he stared the girl in the face. "You look like a corpse come to life. What's the matter?"

"Matter?" replied the girl. "Nothing. What do you look at me so hard for?"

"What is it?" demanded Sikes, grasping her by the arm, and shaking her roughly. "What do you mean? What are you thinking of?"

"Of many things, Bill," replied the girl, shivering and pressing her hands upon her eyes.

"You've caught the fever," said Sikes. "Come and sit

beside me and put on your own face or I'll alter it so that you won't know it again."

The girl obeyed. Sikes, locking her hand in his, fell back upon the pillow, turning his eyes upon her face. They closed, opened again, then closed once more. He fell at last into a deep sleep.

"The drug has taken effect at last," murmured the girl as she rose from the bedside. "I may be too late even now."

She hastily put on her hat and shawl, looking fearfully round from time to time as if she expected every moment to feel the pressure of Sikes's heavy hand upon her shoulder. Then, bending softly over the bed, she kissed the robber's lips, and noiselessly left the house.

Many of the shops were already closing in the back lanes through which she walked on her way to the West End of London. The clock struck ten, increasing her impatience. She tore along the narrow pavement, elbowing the passengers from side to side. When she reached the more wealthy quarter of the town the streets were comparatively deserted. At last she reached her destination, a family hotel in a quiet but handsome street near Hyde Park. After standing for a few seconds as though making up her mind, she entered the hall.

"Now, young woman!" said a smartly-dressed maid, "whom do you want here?"

"Miss Maylie," said Nancy.

The young woman, who had by this time noted her appearance, called a man to answer her.

"Come," said the man, pushing her towards the door. "None of this! Take yourself off."

"You will have to carry me out by force," said the girl violently. "Isn't there anybody here that will carry a simple message from a poor wretch like me?"

"What is it to be?" said the man, softened at last.

"That a young woman earnestly asks to speak to Miss

Maylie alone," said Nancy; "and that if the lady will only hear the first word she has to say, she will know whether to hear her or turn her out of doors."

The man ran upstairs and presently returned and told the woman to follow him. With trembling limbs she followed him to a small room, where he left her and retired.

The girl's life had been wasted in the streets, but there was something of the woman's original nature in her still. When she heard a light step approaching and thought of the wide contrast which the small room would in another moment contain, she felt burdened with the sense of her own deep shame.

She raised her eyes sufficiently to observe that the figure which presented itself was that of a slight and beautiful girl.

"I am the person you inquired for," said the young lady, in a sweet voice. "Tell me why you wished to see me."

The kind tone, the sweet voice, the gentle manner, the absence of any haughtiness, took the girl completely by surprise, and she burst into tears.

"Oh, lady, lady!" said the girl passionately, "if there were more like you, there would be fewer like me."

"Sit down," said Rose. "If you are in poverty or trouble I shall be truly glad to help you if I can. Sit down."

"Let me stand, lady," said the girl, still weeping, "and do not speak to me so kindly till you know me better. Is that door shut?"

"Yes," said Rose. "Why?"

"Because," said the girl, "I am about to put my life, and the lives of others, in your hands. I am the girl that dragged little Oliver back to old Fagin's on the night he went out from the house in Pentonville."

"You!" said Rose Maylie.

"I, lady!" replied the girl. "I am the infamous creature

you have heard of, that lives among thieves and that has never known any better life. Do not mind shrinking openly from me. The poorest women fall back as I make my way along the crowded pavement."

"What dreadful things these are!" said Rose.

"Thank Heaven upon your knees, dear lady," cried the girl, "that you had friends to care for you in your childhood, and that you were never in the midst of cold and hunger and drunkenness as I have been from my cradle."

"I pity you!" said Rose in a broken voice. "It breaks my heart to hear you!"

"Heaven bless you for your goodness!" said the girl. "I have stolen away from those who would surely murder me, if they knew I had been here, to tell you what I have overheard. Do you know a man called Monks?"

"No," said Rose. "I never heard the name."

"He knows you," replied the girl, "and knew you were here, for it was by hearing him speak about the place that I found out where you are. Some time ago, and soon after Oliver was put into your house on the night of the robbery, I overheard a conversation between this man and Fagin in the dark. I found out that Monks had seen Oliver accidentally with two of our boys on the day we first lost him and had known him directly to be the same child that he was watching for, though I couldn't make out why. Monks promised Fagin a sum of money if Oliver was got back; and he was to have more for making him a thief."

"For what purpose?" asked Rose.

"I couldn't find out; I had to escape discovery, for he had caught sight of my shadow on the wall as I listened. I saw him no more till last night."

"And what happened then?"

"I'll tell you, lady. Last night he came again. Again they went upstairs, and I, wrapping myself up so that my shadow should not betray me, again listened at the door.

89

The first words I heard Monks say were these: 'So the only proof of the boy's identity lie at the bottom of the river, and the old woman that received them from his mother is rotting in her coffin.'"

"What is all this?" said Rose.

"The truth, lady, though it comes from my lips," replied the girl. "Then he said that if he could take the boy's life without bringing his own neck in danger, he would; but as he couldn't, he'd be upon the watch to meet him at every turn in life and harm him yet. 'In short, Fagin,' he says, 'Jew as you are, you never laid such snares as I'll lay for my young brother, Oliver.'"

"His brother!" exclaimed Rose.

"Those were his words," said Nancy, glancing uneasily round, haunted by a vision of Sikes. "And now it is growing late, and I have to reach home without suspicion of having been on such an errand as this. I must be back quickly."

"But what can I do?" said Rose. "To what use can I turn this information? Back! Why do you wish to return to companions you paint in such terrible colours? If you repeat this information to a gentleman whom I know, you can be put in some place of safety without delay."

"I wish to go back," said the girl. "I must go back because—how can I tell such things to an innocent lady like you—because among the men I have told you of, there is one I can't leave; no, not even to be saved from the life I am leading now."

"Oh!" said the girl, "do not turn a deaf ear to my request. Do hear my words and let me save you yet."

"Lady," cried the girl, sinking on her knees, "dear, sweet lady, you are the first that ever blessed me with such words as these, and if I had heard them years ago, they might have turned me from a life of sin and sorrow; but it is too late, too late!"

"It is never too late for repentance," said Rose.

"It is," cried the girl; "I cannot leave him now! I could not be the cause of his death. If I told others what I have told you, he would be sure to die. I must go back. Whether it is God's punishment for the wrong I have done, I do not know; but I am drawn back to him in spite of all my suffering and his cruelty and ill-treatment."

"What am I to do?" said Rose. "How can we save Oliver?"

"You must know some kind gentleman that will advise you what to do," answered the girl.

"But where can I find you again when it is necessary?"

"Will you promise me that you will keep my secret and come to meet me alone or with the only other person that knows it, and that I shall not be watched or followed?"

"I promise you solemnly," said Rose.

"Every Sunday night, from eleven until midnight," said the girl, "I will walk on London Bridge if I am alive."

"Stay another moment," said Rose as the girl moved hurriedly towards the door. "Will you return to this gang of robbers, and to this man, when a word can save you? I wish to serve you."

"You would serve me best, lady," replied the girl, "if you could take my life at once. I have felt more grief to think of what I am, tonight, than I ever did before, and it would be something not to die in the hell in which I have lived. God bless you, sweet lady, and send as much happiness on your head as I have brought shame on mine!"

Thus speaking and sobbing aloud, the unhappy creature turned away. Rose Maylie, overpowered by this extraordinary meeting, sank into a chair and tried to collect her wandering thoughts.

Chapter 22

Mr Grimwig's peculiar behaviour

The Maylies had come to London to spend three days only, before departing for some weeks to a distant part of the coast.

Rose was in a difficult situation. She was anxious to penetrate the mystery in which Oliver's history was enveloped, and yet at the same time she could not break her promise of secrecy to the miserable woman who had confided in her.

She was in this restless condition the morning after Nancy's mysterious visit when Oliver came into the room in breathless haste and excitement. On enquiring the cause of his agitation Oliver told her that he had seen the gentleman who had been so good to him—Mr Brownlow—getting out of a coach. The boy was shedding tears of delight as he told the story; he had found out his address.

"Look here," said Oliver, opening a scrap of paper, "here it is; here's where he lives, I'm going there directly! Oh, dear me, dear me! What shall I do when I see him, again?"

Rose read the address, which was in the Strand, and very soon determined upon making use of that discovery.

"Quick!" she said. "Tell them to fetch a carriage, and be ready to go with me. I will take you there directly; I will only tell my aunt that we are going out for an hour, and be ready as soon as you are."

In less than five minutes they were on their way to Mr Brownlow's. When they arrived there, Rose left Oliver in the coach, under pretence of preparing the old gentleman to receive him; and sending up her card by the servant, requested to see Mr Brownlow on very urgent business.

The servant soon returned to beg that she would walk upstairs; she followed him into an upper room and was presented to Mr Brownlow, who was sitting with his old friend, Mr Grimwig.

Rose told Mr Brownlow that he had once shown great kindness to a young boy who was a dear friend of hers and added that she was sure he would take an interest in hearing of him again.

"Indeed!" said Mr Brownlow.

"Oliver Twist, you knew him as," replied Rose.

The words no sooner escaped her lips than Mr Grimwig, who had been reading a large book that lay on the table, upset it with a great crash, and falling back in his chair gave an exclamation of great wonder. Mr Brownlow was no less surprised, although his astonishment was not expressed in the same odd manner. He drew his chair near to Miss Maylie's and said:

"Do me the favour, my dear young lady, to leave entirely out of the question that kindness of which you speak; and if you can produce any evidence which will alter the unfavourable opinion I once had of that poor child, in Heaven's name let me have it."

"A bad one! I'll eat my head if he is not a bad one," growled Mr Grimwig.

"He is a child of a noble nature and a warm heart," said Rose, colouring; "and he has feelings which would do honour to many six times his age."

"I'm only sixty-one," said Mr Grimwig, "and as Oliver is twelve years old at least I don't see the sense of your remark."

"Do not mind what he says, Miss Maylie," said Mr Brownlow; "he does not mean what he says."

"Yes, he does," growled Mr Grimwig.

"No, he does not," said Mr Brownlow, his anger rising as he spoke.

"He'll eat his head if he doesn't," growled Mr Grimwig.

"He would deserve to have it knocked off, if he does," said Mr Brownlow.

"And he'd like to see any man offer to do it," replied Mr Grimwig, knocking his stick upon the floor.

Having gone thus far in their quarrel, the two gentlemen took snuff and afterwards shook hands, according to their custom.

"Now, Miss Maylie, to return to the subject in which you are so much interested. Let me know what information you have of this child."

Rose at once told him all that had happened to Oliver since he left Mr Brownlow's house, adding that Oliver's only sorrow, for some months past, had been that he could not meet with his former benefactor and friend.

"Thank God!" said the old gentleman. "This is great happiness to me, great happiness. But you haven't told me where he is now, Miss Maylie. Why haven't you brought him with you?"

"He is waiting in a coach at the door," replied Rose.

"At this door!" cried the old gentleman, hurrying out of the room and down the stairs without another word.

When he had gone Mr Grimwig rose from his chair and limped as fast as he could up and down the room at least a dozen times, and then, stopping suddenly before Rose, kissed her without the slightest warning.

"Hush!" he said, as the young lady rose in some alarm at this unusual behaviour. "Don't be afraid. I'm old enough to be your grandfather. You're a sweet girl. I like you. Here they are!"

Mr Brownlow returned, accompanied by Oliver, whom Mr Grimwig received very kindly.

"There is somebody else who should not be forgotten," said Mr Brownlow, ringing the bell. "Send Mrs Bedwin here, if you please."

The old housekeeper came quickly and stood at the door, awaiting orders.

"Why, you get blinder every day, Bedwin," said Mr Brownlow. "Put on your glasses and see if you can't find out what you were wanted for, will you?"

The old lady began to search in her pockets for her glasses. But Oliver could wait no more: he sprang into her arms.

"God be good to me!" cried the old nurse, embracing him; "it is my innocent boy!"

"My dear old nurse!" cried Oliver.

"He would come back—I knew he would," said the old woman, holding him in her arms. "How well he looks, and how like a gentleman's son he is dressed again! Where have you been, this long, long while? Ah! the same sweet face, but not so pale; the same soft eye, but not so sad."

Leaving her with Oliver, Mr Brownlow led the way into another room; and there heard from Rose a full account of her meeting with Nancy, and readily promised to consider what should be done.

Then Rose and Oliver returned home.

Chapter 23

The Artful Dodger gets into trouble

Fagin the Jew was in his den, together with his pupils. But the Artful Dodger was not among them; the police had accused him of attempting to pick a pocket, and finding a silver snuff-box on him, they arrested him. Fagin was anxious about him: for the police knew what a clever fellow the Dodger was, and they were sure to bring strong evidence against him. Fagin expected he would be banished for life. One of the boys was sent to attend the trial in order to give a full account of it to Fagin.

The Dodger came into the court-room with the coat sleeves turned up as usual, his left hand in his pocket and his hat in his right hand. Taking his place in the dock he requested to know "what he was placed in that shameful situation for".

"Hold your tongue, will you?" said the jailer.

"I'm an Englishman, ain't I?" answered the Dodger. "Where are my rights?"

"You'll get your rights soon enough," said the jailer, "and pepper with 'em."

"We'll see what the Secretary of State for Home Affairs has got to say about that," replied Mr Dawkins. "Now then! What is this business? I hope that the magistrates won't keep me too long while they read the paper, for I've got an appointment with a gentleman in the City, and I, I'm a man of my word, and very punctual in business matters; he'll go away if I ain't there in time, and then perhaps there will be an action for damages against those who are keeping me away."

The spectators laughed heartily at this.

"Silence there!" cried the jailer.

"What is this?" asked one of the magistrates.

"A pickpocketing case, your worship."

"Has the boy ever been here before?"

"He ought to have been, many times," replied the jailer. "I know him pretty well, your worship."

"Oh! you know me, do you?" cried the Artful, making a note of the statement. "Very good. That's a case of defamation of character, anyway."

Here there was another laugh, and another cry of "Silence".

"Now then, where are the witnesses?" said the clerk.

"Ah! that's right," added the Dodger. "Where are they? I should like to see them."

This wish was immediately fulfilled, for a policeman stepped forward who had seen the prisoner pick the pocket of a gentleman, and when he was arrested and searched a silver snuff-box, with the owner's name on the lid, was found upon his person.

"Have you anything to ask this witness, boy?" said the magistrate.

"No," replied the Dodger, "not here, for this isn't a court of justice; and besides, my lawyer is having breakfast this morning with the Vice-President of the House of Commons. But I shall have something to say elsewhere and I'll——"

"There! Take him away," interrupted the magistrate.

"Come on," said the jailer.

"Oh, I'll come on," replied the Dodger, brushing his hat with the palm of his hand. "Ah! (to the magistrate) it's no use your looking frightened: I won't show any mercy, my fine fellows. I wouldn't be you for anything! I wouldn't go free, now, if you were to fall down on your knees and ask me. Here, carry me off to prison! Take me away!"

With these words the Dodger allowed himself to be led off by the collar, threatening to make a parliamentary business of it.

Having seen him locked up by himself in a little cell, Fagin's boy hastened back to his master to give him the news that the Dodger was doing full justice to his upbringing and making for himself a glorious reputation.

Chapter 24

Nancy keeps her promise

It was Sunday night, and the bell of the nearest church struck the hour. Sikes and the Jew were talking, but they paused to listen. The girl looked up from the low seat on which she lay, and listened too. Eleven.

Nancy put on her hat and was leaving the room.

" Hallo! " cried Sikes. " Where are you going to, Nancy, at this time of night? "

" Not far."

" What answer's that? " returned Sikes. " Where are you going? "

" I don't know where," replied the girl.

" Then I do," said Sikes obstinately. " Nowhere. Sit down."

" I'm not well. I told you that before," answered the girl. " I want a breath of air."

" Put your head out of the window," replied Sikes.

" There's not enough there," said the girl. " I want it in the street."

" Then you won't have it," replied Sikes, rising and locking the door. Pulling her hat from her head he threw it on the top of an old cupboard. " Now stop quietly where you are, will you? "

" Let me go," said the girl, kneeling on the floor. " Bill, let me go for only one hour."

" Cut my limbs off one by one! " cried Sikes, seizing her roughly by the arm, " if I don't think the girl is mad. Get up."

" Not till you let me go—never, never! " screamed the girl. Sikes looked on, for a moment, and suddenly seized both her hands and dragged her into a small room. He threw her into a chair and held her down by force. She struggled and begged by turns until twelve o'clock had struck, and then, wearied and exhausted, she became quiet. Sikes left her to recover at leisure and rejoined Fagin.

"Whew!" said the housebreaker, wiping the sweat from his face. "What a strange girl she is!"

"You may say that, Bill," replied Fagin thoughtfully. "You may say that."

Fagin walked towards his home, intent upon the thoughts that were working within his brain. The girl's altered manner and her impatience to leave home that night at a particular hour had made him think that Nancy, weary of the housebreaker's cruelty, had found a new friend. Such a new friend would be valuable to him, and must be secured without delay.

Before he had reached his home he had made his plans. He would have Nancy watched and discover the object of her new affection.

A week passed: it was Sunday night again. The church clocks struck three quarters past eleven, as two figures appeared on London Bridge. One, which advanced with a rapid step, was that of a woman who looked eagerly about her as though in search of some expected object. The other figure was that of a man, who followed her at some distance, walking in the deepest shadow he could find. Thus they crossed the bridge. At the other side, the woman, apparently disappointed in her search, turned back. The movement was sudden, but her pursuer quickly concealed himself. At nearly the middle of the bridge, she stopped. The man stopped too.

Two minutes later, a young lady, accompanied by a grey-haired gentleman, descended from a carriage within a short distance of the bridge and, having dismissed the carriage, walked straight towards it. They had scarcely set foot upon its pavement when the girl started, and made straight towards them.

They uttered an exclamation of surprise when she suddenly joined them, and stopped; but Nancy said hurriedly: "Not here; I am afraid to speak to you here. Come away—out of the public road—down those steps!"

When the man who was secretly following Nancy heard these words, and saw her pointing to the steps, he hastened there unobserved and hid in a dark turning in the flight of steps. Presently he heard the sound of footsteps, and voices almost close at his ear. He drew himself straight upright against the wall, and scarcely breathed, listening attentively.

"This is far enough," said a voice, which was evidently that of the gentleman. "I will not allow the young lady to go any farther. Now, for what purpose have you brought us to this strange, gloomy place?"

"I told you before," replied Nancy, "that I was afraid to speak to you there. I don't know why it is, but I have such a fear and dread upon me tonight that I can hardly stand."

"A fear of what?" asked the gentleman, who seemed to pity her.

"I scarcely know of what," replied the girl. "I wish I did. Horrible thoughts of death and blood have been upon me all day."

"You were not here last Sunday night," said the gentleman.

"I couldn't come," replied Nancy; "I was kept by force."

"By whom?"

"Him that I told the young lady of before."

"You were not suspected of holding any communication with anybody on the subject which has brought us here tonight, I hope?" asked the old gentleman.

"No," replied the girl, shaking her head.

"Good," said the gentleman. "Now listen to me. This young lady has communicated to me, and to some other friends who can be safely trusted, what you told her nearly a fortnight ago. I am inclined to trust you, and therefore I tell you without reserve that we are determined to force the secret, whatever it is, from this man Monks. Put Monks into my hands, and leave him to me to deal with."

"What if he turns against Fagin and the others?"

"I promise you that in that case, if the truth is forced from him, there the matter will rest; the others shall go free."

"And if it is not?" asked the girl.

"Then," said the gentleman, "this Fagin shall not be brought to justice without your consent."

"Have I the lady's promise for that?" asked the girl.

"You have," replied Rose. "My true and faithful promise."

"Monks would never learn how you knew what you know?" said the girl after a short pause.

"Never," replied the gentleman.

"I have been a liar, and among liars, since I was a little child," said the girl, after another pause, "but I will take your words."

Then, in a very low voice, she started to describe the public-house where Monks was to be found, the best position from which to watch it without being observed, and the night and hour on which Monks was most in the habit of frequenting it. "He is tall," said the girl, "and a strongly built man; and as he walks, he constantly looks over his shoulder first on one side, and then on the other. His eyes are deeply sunk in his head, and his face is dark, like his hair and eyes. I think that's all I can give you to know him by. Wait, though," she added. "Upon his throat there is——"

"A broad red mark, like a burn?" cried the gentleman.

"How's this?" said the girl. "You know him!"

The young lady uttered a cry of surprise, and for a few moments they were so still that the listener could distinctly hear them breathe.

"I think I do," said the gentleman, breaking the silence. "I should, by your description. We shall see. Many people are extraordinarily like each other. It may not be the same man. And now, young woman, you have given us most valuable assistance, and I wish to reward you for it. What can I do for you?"

"Nothing," replied Nancy.

"You must tell me," said the old gentleman, very kindly.

"Nothing, sir," replied the girl, weeping. "You can do nothing to help me. I am past all hope, indeed."

"It is true that the past has been wasted, but you may hope for the future. I do not say that it is in our power to offer you peace of heart and mind, for that must come as you seek it. But we can send you to a quiet place of shelter, either in England, or, if you fear to remain here, in some foreign country. Before dawn you shall be placed as entirely beyond the reach of your former companions as if you were to disappear from the earth this moment. Come! I would not have you go back to exchange one word with such companions. Leave them, while you have the chance."

"I can't, sir," said the girl, after a short struggle. "I am chained to my old life. I hate it with all my heart, now, but I cannot leave it. I must have gone too far to turn back. I must go home."

"Home!" repeated the young lady.

"Home, lady," answered the girl. "Let us part. I shall be watched or seen. Go! Go! If I have done you any service, all that I ask is that you leave me and let me go my way alone."

"It is useless," said the gentleman, with a sigh. "We are endangering her safety, perhaps, by staying here."

The two figures of the young lady and her companion soon afterwards appeared upon the bridge. The old gentleman drew her arm through his and led her away. As they disappeared the girl sank down upon one of the stairs and cried with bitter tears.

After a time she arose and with unsteady steps ascended to the road. The astonished spy remained motionless for some minutes afterwards, and having made certain that he was again alone, crept slowly from his hiding-place and, reaching the top, he ran towards the Jew's house as fast as his legs could carry him.

Chapter 25

Fatal consequences

It was nearly two hours before daybreak when Fagin sat watching in his old den, with face so pale and eyes so red that he looked less like a man than like a ghost.

Stretched upon a mattress on the floor fast asleep lay the young spy who had followed Nancy and overheard her secret conversation below London Bridge. Towards him the old man sometimes directed his eyes for an instant, and then brought them back. He was deeply occupied with his evil thoughts. His plan of discovering Nancy's new lover had failed; for she had none. He was full of hatred for her because she dared to have dealings with strangers, and he distrusted the sincerity of her refusal to yield him up. He was full of a deadly fear of being discovered.

He sat still for quite a long time until at last his quick ear seemed to be attracted by a footstep in the street. The bell rang gently; he crept to the door and presently returned with Bill Sikes, who carried a bundle under one arm.

"There!" he said, laying the bundle on the table. "Take care of that, and do the most you can with it. It's been trouble enough to get."

Fagin laid his hand upon the bundle and, locking it in the cupboard, sat down again without speaking. But he did not take his eyes off the robber, for an instant.

"What is it now?" growled Sikes. "What do you look at me like that for? Are you gone mad?"

"No, no," replied Fagin, "but I've got something to tell you that won't please you."

"What is it?" said the robber. "Speak, will you! Or if you don't, it shall be for lack of breath. Open your mouth and say what you've got to say in plain words. Out with it, you old dog, out with it!"

Fagin made no answer, but bending over the sleeper he pulled him into a sitting position.

"Tell me that again . . . once again, just for him to hear," said the Jew, pointing to Sikes as he spoke.

"Tell you what?" asked the boy sleepily.

"That about . . . *Nancy*," said Fagin, holding Sikes by the wrist, as if to prevent his leaving the house before he had heard enough. "You followed her?"

"Yes."

"To London Bridge?"

"Yes."

"Where she met two people?"

"So she did."

"A gentleman and a lady that she had gone to see before, who asked her to give up all her friends, and Monks first, which she did, and to tell her about the place where we met, which she did. She told it all, every word, did she not?" cried Fagin, half mad with fury.

"That's right," replied the boy. "That's just what it was!"

"What did they say about last Sunday?"

"They asked her," said the boy, "why she didn't come last Sunday, as she promised. She said she couldn't."

"Why . . . why? Tell him that."

"Because she was forcibly kept at home by Bill," replied the boy.

"Hell's fire!" cried Sikes, breaking fiercely from the Jew. "Let me go!"

Pushing the old man away from him, he rushed from the room and darted up the stairs.

"Bill, Bill," cried Fagin, following him hastily. "A word. Only a word."

"Let me out," said Sikes. "Don't speak to me; it's not safe. Let me out, I say!"

"Hear me speak a word," said Fagin, laying his hand upon the lock. "You won't be . . . too . . . violent, Bill? I mean, not too violent for safety. Be cunning, Bill, and not too bold."

Sikes made no reply, but, pulling open the door, he rushed into the silent streets.

Without one pause, or a moment's consideration, and looking straight before him with savage determination, the robber rushed headlong to his home. Opening the door softly he stepped lightly up the stairs, and entering his own room, double-locked the door and pushed a heavy table against it.

The girl was lying half-dressed upon the bed. He had roused her from her sleep, for she raised herself with a hurried and frightened look.

"Get up!" said the man.

"It *is* you, Bill!" said the girl, with an expression of pleasure at his return.

"It is," was the reply. "Get up."

There was a candle burning, but the man hastily drew it from the candlestick and threw it into the fireplace. Seeing the faint light of early day outside, the girl rose to undraw the curtain.

"Let it be," said Sikes. "There's light enough for what I've got to do."

"Bill," said the girl, in the low voice of alarm, "why do you look like this at me?"

The robber stood regarding her for a few seconds, breathing quickly, then, grasping her by the hand and throat, dragged her into the middle of the room, and placed his heavy hand upon her mouth.

"Bill, Bill!" gasped the girl, struggling with the strength of deadly fear. "I won't scream or cry. Hear me . . . speak to me . . . tell me what I have done!"

"You know, you she-devil!" returned the robber. "You were watched tonight; every word you said was heard."

"Then spare my life for the love of Heaven, as I spared yours," said the girl, throwing her arms around him. "Bill, dear Bill, you cannot have the heart to kill me. Oh! think of all I have given up, only tonight, for you. You *shall* have time to think, and save yourself from this crime. I will not loosen my hold, you cannot throw me off. Bill, Bill, for dear God's sake, for your own, for mine, stop before you spill my blood. I have been true to you, upon my soul I have!"

The housebreaker freed one arm and grasped his pistol. Even in the midst of his fury he realised that is would be dangerous to fire. He beat it twice with all his force upon the upturned face that almost touched his own.

She fell nearly blinded with the blood that rained down from a deep cut in her forehead. But raising herself with difficulty on her knees, she breathed one prayer for mercy to her Maker.

Hers was a terrible figure to look upon. The murderer

stepped backward to the wall and, shutting out the sight with his hand, seized a heavy stick and struck her down.

Chapter 26

The flight of Sikes

Of all bad deeds that, under cover of the darkness, had been committed within the bounds of London since night hung over it, that was the worst. The sun that brings back, not light alone, but new life and hope to man, burst upon the crowded city, and lighted up the room where the murdered woman lay. Sikes tried to shut the light out, but it would stream in. If the sight had been a terrible one in the dull morning, what was it now, in all that brilliant light!

He had not moved; he had been afraid to stir. There had been a moan and a motion of the hand; and with terror added to rage, he had struck and struck again. Once he threw a rug over it, but it was terrible to fancy the eyes, and imagine them moving towards him.

He struck a light, lit a fire and threw the heavy stick into it. He washed himself, and rubbed his clothes; there were spots that would not be removed, but he cut the pieces out, and burnt them. How those stains were scattered about the room! The very feet of the dog were bloody.

All this time he had never once turned his back upon the corpse; no, not for a moment. Having completed his preparations and cleaned the dog's feet, he moved backward towards the door, dragging the dog with him, lest he should soil his feet again and carry out new evidence of the crime into the streets. He shut the door softly, locked it, took the key, and left the house.

He crossed over, and looked up at the window, to be sure that nothing was visible from the outside. There was the curtain still drawn, which she would have opened to admit the light she never saw again. The corpse lay nearly under there. He whistled to the dog, and walked rapidly away.

It was nine o'clock at night when the man, quite tired out, and the dog, walking lamely from the unaccustomed exercise, turned down a hill and walking wearily along a little village street, crept into a small public-house. There was a fire burning, and some villagers were drinking before it. They made room for the stranger, but he sat down in the farthest corner, and ate and drank alone, or rather with his dog, to whom he cast a bit of food from time to time.

The conversation of the men turned upon the neighbouring land, and farmers. There was nothing to attract attention, or arouse alarm in this. The robber, after paying his account, sat silent and unnoticed in his corner, and had almost dropped asleep, when he was half awakened by the noisy entrance of a newcomer.

This was a curious pedlar who travelled about the country on foot to sell razors, cheap perfumes, medicine for dogs and horses and such like articles which he carried in a box hanging on his back. Having eaten his supper, he opened his box of treasures, hoping to find some buyers.

"And what is that stuff? Good to eat, Harry?" asked a countryman, pointing to some cakes in a corner.

"This," said the fellow, producing one, "is the infallible and invaluable composition for removing all sorts of stain, rust, dirt or spots from all sorts of stuff, silk, woollen or linen. Wine-stains, fruit-stains, beer-stains, water-stains, paint-stains, any stains, all come out at one rub with this infallible and invaluable composition. If a lady stains her honour, she has only need to swallow one cake and she's cured at once . . . for it's poison. One penny a square. With all these virtues, one penny a square!"

There were two buyers directly, and more of the listeners plainly hesitated. The pedlar, observing this, continued to talk.

"It's all bought up as fast as it can be made," said the fellow. "There are fourteen factories always working upon it, and they can't make it fast enough. One penny a square! Wine-stains, fruit-stains, beer-stains, water-stains, paint-stains, mud-stains, blood-stains! Here is a stain upon the hat of a gentleman present, that I'll take clean out, before he can order me a pint beer."

"Hah!" cried Sikes, starting up. "Give that back."

"I'll take it clear out, sir," replied the man, winking to the company, "before you can come across the room to get it. Gentlemen all, observe the dark stain upon this gentleman's hat, no wider than a shilling, but thicker than a half-crown. Whether it is a wine-stain, fruit-stain, beer-stain, water-stain, paint-stain or blood-stain . . ."

The man got no further, for Sikes with an oath overthrew the table, and tearing the hat from him, burst out of the house.

The murderer, finding that he was not followed, and that they most probably considered him some drunken ill-tempered fellow, turned back up the village. As he walked up the street he recognised the mail-coach from London standing at the little post-office. He almost knew what was to come, but he crossed over and listened.

The post master came out with the letter-bag which he handed to the guard.

"Anything new in town?" he asked.

"No, nothing that I know of," the guard replied. "The price of corn is up a little. I heard talk of a murder, too."

"That's quite true," said a gentleman inside the coach,

who was looking out of the window. "And a dreadful murder it was."

"Was it, sir?" said the guard. "Man or woman?"

"A woman," replied the gentleman. "They say . . ."

Sikes did not wait to hear any more. He took the road leading out of the village, and as he left it behind him and plunged into the solitude and darkness of the road, he felt a great fear creeping upon him. Every object before him, still or moving, took the likeness of some fearful thing. But these fears were nothing compared to the thought that haunted him of the girl's murdered body following at his heels. He could trace its shadow in the gloom, and note how stiff and solemn it seemed to move. He could hear the rustling of its garments, and every breath of wind came laden with that last low cry. If he stopped, it did the same. If he ran, it followed.

At times he turned, with a desperate determination to beat this ghost off. But the hair rose on his head, and his blood stood still, for it had turned with him and was behind him then. He had kept it before him that morning, but it was behind him now . . . always. He leaned his back against a hedge, and felt that it stood above him. He threw himself upon the road. At his head it stood, silent and still.

Let no man talk of murderers escaping justice. There were twenty violent deaths in each minute of that agony of fear.

He came to a shed in a field that offered shelter for the night. He could not walk on till daylight came again; he went in and lay down close to the wall—to suffer new agony.

For now, a vision came before him even more terrible than that from which he had escaped. Those widely staring eyes, lifeless and glassy, appeared in the midst of darkness. There were but two, but they were everywhere. If he shut

E

out the sight, there came the room with every well-known object, each in its accustomed place. The body was in its place, and its eyes were as he saw them when he stole away. He got up and rushed out into the field. The figure was behind him. He re-entered the shed, and lay down once more. The eyes were there.

And there he remained in such terror as none but he can know, trembling in every limb and the cold sweat starting from every pore, until morning dawned again. Suddenly he made the desperate decision to go back to London.

"There's somebody to speak to there, at all events," he thought. "A good hiding-place, too. They'll never expect to catch me there, after I had escaped to the country. I could remain in hiding there for a week or so, and then, forcing some money out of Fagin, get abroad to France. I'll risk it."

He acted upon this decision without delay, and, choosing the most deserted roads, began his journey back to London, resolving to enter it when night had fallen.

The dog, though. If any description of him were out, it would not be forgotten that the dog was missing, and had probably gone with him. This might lead to his arrest as he passed along the streets. He resolved to drown him, and walked on, looking about for a pond; he picked up a heavy stone and tied it to his handkerchief as he went.

The animal looked up into his master's face while he was making these preparations, as if he understood by instinct their purpose, and he followed a little further back than usual. When his master came to the edge of a pond and looked round to call him, he stopped dead.

"Do you hear me call? Come here!" cried Sikes.

The animal came up from the very force of habit; but as Sikes bent to tie the handkerchief to his throat he uttered a low growl and started away.

"Come back!" said the robber.

The dog wagged his tail, but did not move. Sikes called him again. The dog advanced, retreated, paused an instant, turned and ran away at his hardest speed.

The man whistled again and again, and sat down and waited in the expectation that he would return. But no dog appeared, and at length he resumed his journey.

Chapter 27

Monks and Mr Brownlow meet at last

It was getting dark when Mr Brownlow descended from a coach at his own door and knocked softly. The door being opened, a strong man got out of the coach and stood at one side of the steps, while another man, who had been seated on the coachman's seat, dismounted too, and stood upon the other side. At a sign from Mr Brownlow, they helped out a third man, and taking him between them, hurried him into the house. This man was Monks.

They walked in the same manner upstairs without speaking, and Mr Brownlow led the way into a back room. At the door of this room Monks stopped. The two men looked to the old gentleman as for instructions.

"If he hesitates or refuses to obey you," said Mr Brownlow, "drag him into the street, call the police and let them arrest him as a criminal."

"How dare you say that of me?" asked Monks.

"How dare you urge me to it, young man?" said Mr Brownlow. "Are you mad enough to leave this house? Release him. There, sir, you are free to go, and we to follow. But I warn you that the instant you set foot in the street

I will have you arrested on a charge of fraud and robbery."

"By what authority am I kidnapped in the street, and brought here by these dogs?" asked Monks, looking from one to the other of the men who stood beside him.

"By mine," replied Mr Brownlow. "If you complain of being deprived of your liberty, ask for the protection of the law. I will appeal to the law too. But do not ask me for mercy when it is too late."

Monks was plainly alarmed. He hesitated.

"You will decide quickly," said Mr Brownlow, firmly. "If you want me to charge you in public, you know the way. If not, and you appeal to my forgiveness and the mercy of those whom you have deeply injured, seat yourself, without a word, in that chair. It has waited for you two whole days."

"Is there . . . no middle course?" asked Monks.

"None."

Monks looked at the old gentleman, with an anxious eye; but reading in his face nothing but a firm determination, he walked into the room and sat down.

"Lock the door on the outside," said Mr Brownlow to the two men, "and come when I ring."

The men obeyed, and the two were left alone together.

"This is pretty treatment, sir," said Monks, throwing down his hat and cloak, "from my father's oldest friend."

"It is because I was your father's oldest friend, young man," returned Mr Brownlow, "it is because he knelt with me beside the death-bed of his only sister when he was yet a boy, on the morning that would have made her my young wife; it is because of all this that I am moved to treat you gently now . . . yes, Edward Leeford, even now . . . and blush for your own wickedness, you who bear the name."

"What is the name to me?" asked Monks.

"Nothing," replied Mr Brownlow, "nothing to you. But

it was *hers*, and even at this distance of time brings back to me, an old man, the thrill which I once felt when I heard it. I am glad you have changed it."

"This is all very well," said Monks, "but what do you want with me?"

"You have a brother," said Mr Brownlow, "the whisper of whose name in your ear when I came behind you in the street was enough to make you accompany me here, in wonder and alarm."

"I have no brother," replied Monks. "You know I was an only child. Why do you talk to me of brothers?"

"I know," said Mr Brownlow, "that of the wretched marriage into which family pride and ambition forced your unhappy father you were the only child. But I also know that their marriage was a slow torture to both parties until at last they were separated."

"Well," said Monks, "they were separated, and what of that?"

"When they had been separated for some time," returned Mr Brownlow, "your father fell among new friends. *This*, at least, you knew already."

"Not I," replied Monks, turning away his eyes and beating his foot upon the ground, as a man who is determined to deny everything. "Not I."

"Your manner assures me that you have never forgotten it," returned Mr Brownlow. "I speak of fifteen years ago, when you were not more than eleven years old, and your father but one-and-thirty. These new friends were a retired naval officer whose wife had died and left him a daughter, a beautiful creature of nineteen. Your father fell in love passionately with her, and the result of this guilty love was your brother."

"Your tale is a long one," observed Monks, moving restlessly in his chair.

"It is a true tale of grief and trial, young man," returned

Mr Brownlow, "and such tales usually *are* long; if it were one of unmixed joy and happiness, it would be very brief. At length one of your father's rich relations died and left him considerable property. It was necessary that your father should go to Rome, where this rich relation had died. And there your father was seized with illness; he was followed, the moment the news reached Paris, by your mother, who carried you with her. He died the day after her arrival, leaving no will . . . *no will* . . . . so that the whole property fell to her and to you."

Here Monks, who had been listening with eager interest, showed signs of a sudden relief, and wiped his hot face and hands.

"Before he went abroad, and as he passed through London on his way," said Mr Brownlow slowly, and fixing his eyes upon the other's face, "he came to me."

"I never heard of that," interrupted Monks.

"He came to me, and left with me a picture painted by himself of this poor girl, which he did not wish to leave behind, and could not carry forward on his hasty journey. He was worn by anxiety and remorse; talked of ruin and dishonour brought about by himself, and confided to me his intention to sell his property and settle a part of the money on his wife and you and then leave the country and never see it any more. But even from me he kept the confession of the secret fruit of his guilty love. He promised to write and tell me all, and after that to see me once again. Alas! *that* was the last time. I had no letter, and I never saw him again.

"I went," said Mr Brownlow, after a short pause, "to the scene of his unhappy love, resolved to find the poor girl and give her shelter. But the family had left that part of the country a week before. It was by the strong hand of chance that your poor neglected brother was thrown in my way. And when I rescued him from a life of vice and crime

I was struck by his strong similarity to this picture I have spoken of. I need not tell you he was snared away before I knew his history . . ."

"Why not?" asked Monks hastily.

"Because you know it well."

"I!"

"It is no use denying," replied Mr Brownlow. "I shall show you that I know more than that."

"You . . . you . . . can't prove anything against me," said Monks.

"We shall see," returned the old gentleman, with a searching glance. "I lost the boy, and no efforts of mine could recover him. Your mother being dead, I knew that you alone could solve the mystery if anybody could. I searched for you everywhere in London, where I had found you were keeping company with the lowest of criminals. I walked the streets day and night, but until two hours ago all my efforts were fruitless, and I never saw you for an instant."

"And now you do see me," said Monks, rising boldly, "what then? Do you think you can prove your charges against me by a fancied similarity between a miserable child and a badly painted picture? Brother! You don't even know that a child was born; you don't even know that."

"I did not," replied Mr Brownlow, rising too; "but during the last fortnight I have learnt it all. There was a will, which your mother destroyed, leaving the secret and the gain to you at her own death. It contained a reference to some child likely to be the result of this sad connexion. According to the will the child was to inherit all his father's property if he grew up to be a worthy man; if, on the other hand, he became a man of low character like yourself, the property was to be equally shared between you two. The child was born and you accidentally met him; your suspicions were first aroused by his resemblance to your father.

You went to the place of his birth where there were proofs of his origin. Those proofs were destroyed by you, and now, in your own words to your partner the Jew, 'the only proofs of the boy's identity lie at the bottom of the river, and the old woman that received them from the mother is in her grave.' Unworthy son, coward, liar—you who hold your councils with thieves and murderers in dark rooms at night, you, Edward Leeford, do you still challenge me?"

"No, no, no!" replied the coward.

"Every word!" cried the old gentleman, "every word that has passed between you and this villain is known to me. Shadows on the wall have caught your whispers, and brought them to my ear. Murder has been done, to which you were morally if not actually a party."

"No, no," interrupted Monks. "I . . . I . . . know nothing of that; I was going to inquire the truth of the story when you caught me. I didn't know the reason. I thought it was a common quarrel."

"It was the partial revealing of your secrets," said Mr Brownlow, "that was the cause of the murder. And now will you sign a true statement of facts and repeat it before witnesses?"

"I will."

"You must do more than that," said Mr. Brownlow. "You must repair the injury you have done to an innocent child, and carry out your father's will so far as the child is concerned. Then you may go where you please."

While Monks was walking up and down the room, thinking with dark and evil looks, torn by his fears on the one hand and his hatred on the other, the door was hurriedly unlocked, and a gentleman entered the room in great excitement.

"The man will be taken," he cried. "He will be taken tonight!"

"The murderer?" asked Mr Brownlow.

"Yes, yes," replied the other. "His dog has been seen, and there seems little doubt that his master is hiding near by, under cover of darkness. I have spoken to the men who are pursuing him, and they tell me he cannot escape. A reward of a hundred pounds is proclaimed by the government tonight."

"And I will give fifty more," said Mr Brownlow. "What about Fagin? Any news of him?"

"He has not yet been taken, but they're sure to get him."

"Have you made up your mind?" asked Brownlow, in a low voice, of Monks.

"Yes," he replied. "You . . . you . . . will keep my secret?"

"I will, if you sign now a true statement of facts before witnesses and restore to Oliver Twist the money and property you have unlawfully seized from him."

The statement having been duly made and signed by Monks, he was released.

Chapter 28

The end of Sikes

Jacob's Island stands in the Thames, near one of the poorest and dirtiest quarters of London. It is surrounded by a ditch of muddy water six or eight feet deep when the tide is in. The island is deserted; its houses are roofless and empty; the walls are falling down; the windows are windows no more; the chimneys are blackened, but they yield no smoke. The houses have no owners; they are broken open and entered upon by those who have the courage; and there they live, and there they die. They must have powerful reasons for a secret dwelling-place, or be very poor indeed, who seek shelter on Jacob's Island.

In an upper room of one of these houses three men sat in gloomy silence. One of them was Toby Crackit and the others were fellow robbers. They were talking about Fagin, who had been arrested that same afternoon. Suddenly a hurried knocking was heard at the door below.

Toby Crackit went to the window, and shaking all over, drew in his head. There was no need to tell them who it was; his pale face was enough.

"We must let him in," he said, taking up the candle.

Crackit went down to the door, and returned followed by a man with the lower part of his face buried in a handkerchief, and another tied over his head under his hat. He drew them slowly off. White face, sunken eyes, hollow cheeks, beard of three days' growth; it was the very ghost of Sikes.

He drew a chair and sat down. Not a word had been exchanged. He looked from one to another in silence. At last he said:

"Tonight's paper says that Fagin is taken. Is it true, or a lie?"

"True."

They were silent again.

"Damn you all!" said Sikes, passing his hand across his forehead. "Have you nothing to say to me?"

There was an uneasy movement among them, but nobody spoke.

Presently there was a knocking at the door. Crackit left the room and directly came back with Charlie Bates behind him. Sikes sat opposite the door, so that the moment the boy entered the room he saw him.

"Toby," said the boy, shrinking back, as Sikes turned his eyes towards him, "why didn't you tell me this downstairs? Let me go into some other room."

"Charlie," said Sikes, stepping forward. "Don't you . . . don't you know me?"

"Don't come near me," answered the boy, still retreating and looking, with horror in his eyes, upon the murderer's face. "You monster!"

Sikes's eyes sunk gradually to the ground.

"Witness, you three," said the boy, becoming more and more excited as he spoke. "I'm not afraid of him. If they come here after him, I'll give him up; I will. He may kill me for it if he likes, or if he dares, but if I'm here I'll give him up. Murder! Help! Down with him!"

Pouring out these cries the boy actually threw himself, single-handed, upon the strong man, and in the suddenness of his attack brought him heavily to the ground.

The three spectators did not interfere, and the boy and the man rolled on the ground together. But the struggle was too unequal to last long. Sikes had him down, and his knee was on his throat, when Crackit pulled him back with a look of alarm, and pointed to the window. There were lights gleaming below, voices in loud and earnest conversation, the noise of hurried footsteps crossing the nearest wooden bridge. Then came a loud knocking at the door, and a murmur from a thousand angry voices.

"Help!" screamed the boy. "He's here. Break down the door!"

"Open the door of some place where I can lock this screaming child," cried Sikes fiercely; running to and fro and dragging the boy. "That door. Quick!" He threw him in, bolted it, and turned the key. "Is the downstairs door fast?"

"Double-locked and chained," replied Crackit.

"The wood . . . is it strong?"

"Lined with sheet-iron."

"And the windows too?"

"Yes, and the windows."

"Damn you," cried the desperate murderer, throwing open the window and facing the crowd. "Do your worst! I'll cheat you yet!"

There was a cry of rage from the angry crowd. Some shouted to those who were nearest to set the house on fire; others roared to the officers to shoot him dead. Among them all, none showed such fury as a man on horseback who burst through the crowd and cried, "Twenty guineas to the man who brings a ladder!"

The nearest voices took up the cry, and hundreds echoed it. Some called for ladders, some for heavy hammers, and all moved excitedly to and fro, in the darkness below, like a field of corn moved by an angry wind, and joined from time to time in one loud, furious roar.

"The tide," cried the murderer, as he drew back into the room, "was in as I came up. Give me a rope, a long rope. They're all in front. I may drop into the ditch at the back, and escape that way. Give me a rope, or I shall do three more murders and kill myself."

The frightened men pointed to where the ropes were kept. The murderer hastily selected the longest and strongest, and hurried up to the house-top.

All the windows at the back of the house had been long ago bricked up, except a small one in the room where Charlie Bates was locked. And from this window he had never ceased to call on the crowd to guard the back. And thus when the murderer appeared at last on the house-top by the door in the roof, a loud shout declared the fact to those in front, and they immediately began to pour round, pressing upon each other in an unbroken stream.

The murderer crept on the roof and looked down over the low wall. The tide was out, and the ditch a bed of mud.

The crowd had been silent during these few moments, watching his movements and doubtful of his purpose. But as soon as they understood it, and knew it was defeated, they raised a cry of triumph to which all their previous shouting had been whispers.

On pressed the people from the front—on, on, on, in a strong struggling crowd of angry voices, with here and there a torch to light them up, and show them out in their fury. Each little bridge bent beneath the weight of the crowd upon it. It seemed as though the whole city had poured its population out to curse him.

"They have him now," cried a man on the nearest bridge. "Hurrah!" The crowd uncovered their heads and re-echoed the shout.

The man shrank down, thoroughly frightened by the fierceness of the crowd. But then he sprang upon his feet, determined to make one last effort for his life by dropping into the ditch and, at the risk of being choked to death in the mud, trying to creep away in the darkness and confusion.

Roused into new strength and energy, he fastened one end of the rope tightly round the chimney. With the other end he made a running noose. He could let himself down nearly to the ground and he had his knife ready in his hand to cut the rope then and drop.

He put the noose over his head, and was about to place it round his body when suddenly he cried aloud: "The eyes again!" Drawing back as if struck by lightning he lost his balance and dropped from the roof. The noose was on his neck. He fell for five-and-thirty feet. There was a sudden jerk, a terrible shaking of the limbs, and there he hung, with the knife held tightly in his lifeless hand.

Chapter 29

Fagin's last hours

The court was packed with people. Curious eyes looked from every inch of space, and all were fixed upon one man —Fagin. He stood in the dock, with his head thrust forward to enable him to catch every word that fell from the judge's lips as he delivered his speech to the jury. At times, he turned his eyes sharply upon them to observe the effect of the judge's words upon them. At other times he looked towards his lawyer in a silent appeal that he would, even then, say something in his favour. He had scarcely moved since the trial began; and now that the judge ceased to speak, he still remained in the same attitude of close attention as though he listened still.

A slight noise in the court recalled him to himself. Looking round, he saw the members of the jury passing out, to consider their verdict. He looked around him; he could see the people rising above each other to see his face.

At length there was a cry of silence: the jury returned, and passed close by him. He could learn nothing from their faces; they might as well have been of stone. Perfect silence followed—not a breath— "guilty!"

The building rang with a tremendous shout, and another, and another. When silence was restored Fagin was asked if he had anything to say why sentence of death should not be passed upon him. He had resumed his silent attitude; the question was repeated to him twice before he could answer, and then all he could say was that he was an old man—an old man.

They led him out of the court room through another room where some prisoners were awaiting trial, and through a gloomy passage into the interior of the prison.

Here he was searched lest he should have about him some means of killing himself; then he was led to his cell where he was left alone.

He sat down on a stone bench which served for seat and bed, and tried to collect his thoughts. After a while he began to remember a few words of what the judge had said. These gradually fell into their proper places, and by degrees suggested more. In a little while he had the whole speech, almost as it was delivered. To be hanged by the neck till he was dead—that was the end. To be hanged by the neck till he was dead.

As it came on very dark, he began to think of all the men he had known who had died upon the scaffold, some of them through his means. He had seen some of them die, and had joked too, because they died with prayers upon their lips. Some of them might have inhabited that very cell—sat upon that very spot. It was very dark; why didn't they bring a light? He began to beat with his hands on the heavy door of the cell. At length two men appeared, one bearing a candle, which he put into an iron candlestick fixed against the wall, the other dragging in a mattress on which to pass the night, for the prisoner was to be left alone no more.

Saturday night. He had only one night more to live. And as he thought of this, the day broke—Sunday.

The condemned criminal was seated on his bed, rocking himself from side to side, with a face more like that of a trapped beast than that of a man. His mind was wandering to his old life, and he continued to mutter, apparently unconscious of the presence of his jailers:

"Good boy, Charlie—well done! Oliver, too, ha! ha! ha! Quite the gentleman now—quite the . . ."

"Fagin," said the jailer. "Fagin, Fagin! Here's somebody wants to speak to you. Now sir," he said, as Mr Brownlow entered, "tell him what you want, quick, if you please, for he grows worse as the time gets on."

"You have some papers," said Mr. Brownlow, advancing, "which were placed in your hands, for better security, by a man called Monks."

"It's all a lie," replied Fagin. "I haven't any papers."

"For the love of God," said Mr Brownlow solemnly, "do not say that now; tell me where they are. You know that Sikes is dead; that Monks has confessed; that there is no hope of any further gain. Where are those papers?"

"The papers," said Fagin, "are in a canvas bag, in a hole a little way up the chimney in the top front-room."

"Have you nothing else to ask him, sir?" inquired the jailer.

"No, thank you," replied Mr Brownlow.

Chapter 30

Conclusion

The fortunes of those who have figured in this tale are nearly closed. The little that remains is told in a few and simple words.

Mr Brownlow adopted Oliver as his son, and moved with him and the old housekeeper to within a mile of the house of Mrs Maylie and Rose. Thus the only remaining wish of Oliver's warm heart, to be near his friends, was fulfilled.

Monks, still bearing that assumed name, retired with the share of the money Mr Brownlow allowed him to keep to a distant part of the New World. Here he quickly wasted his wealth and once more fell into his old life of crime and ended in prison, where he died. In the same manner died the chief remaining members of Fagin's band. But Charlie Bates, shocked by Sikes's crime, turned his back upon his past life, and succeeded at last in becoming a farmer's boy and is now the merriest young labourer in the south of England.

Mr Grimwig and Dr Losberne became very close friends. Mr Brownlow often joked with Grimwig and reminded him of the night on which they sat with the watch between them, waiting for Oliver's return. But Mr Grimwig always insisted that Oliver *did not come back*. At this the two old gentlemen laughed aloud.

Mr and Mrs Bumble, deprived of their posts as masters of the workhouse, were gradually reduced to great poverty, and finally became paupers in that very same workhouse of which they had once been masters. As to Mr Giles and Brittles, they still remain in their old posts, although the former is bald, and the last-named boy quite grey. They divide their attentions so equally between the households of the Maylies and Mr Brownlow that to this day the villagers have never been able to discover to which household they properly belong.

Glossary

The abbreviations used are: n. = noun; v. = verb; adj. = adjective;
p.t. = past tense; esp. = especially

A

adjust: (1) to set right; (2) to make something fit.
advance: advanced in years=old.
affected: deeply affected=with feelings of great sadness.
affirmative: nodded in the affirmative=moved his head in a way which meant 'Yes'.
agitated: excited; (n.) *agitation.*
agony: great pain or suffering.
agreeable: (1) pleasing; (2) ready to agree.
air: manner, appearance: e.g. *with the air of a stranger*=looking like a stranger;
    with a determined air=looking determined.
alarming: frightening.
all: all but=almost, nearly.
alter: change.
alternate: one after the other.
amaze: astonish; (n.) *amazement.*
amiable: friendly.
anchor: (v.) to fix a ship in one place with *an anchor* (=instrument let down to
    the bottom of the sea to prevent a ship from moving).
appearances: to all appearances=so far as can be seen.
apprentice: one who has promised to serve a master for a number of years in order
    to learn his trade; *apprenticeship*=the state of being an apprentice.
arouse: waken; *arouse suspicion*=to cause others to suspect something.
artful: clever and deceiving.
ascend: to go up.
assent: (n.) agreement.
aye: yes.

B

bacon: salted meat from the back and sides of a pig.
bald: without hair on the head.
bandage: (v.) to tie up in pieces of cloth.
banish: to send away from the country as punishment.
barrier: a rough fence across a path to prevent people from passing.
behalf: on his behalf=for the purpose of helping him.
bench: the bench=a judge's position.
benefactor: one who does good to others.
blank: missing word.
blind: see Window-blind.

bloom: *the bloom of womanhood*=the beauty of woman at its best.
blush: to become red in the face with shyness or shame.
bolt: bar used to fasten a door.
bonnet: hat tied on the head with strings.
bounds: boundaries, limits.
box: *a box on the ear*=a blow.
bracelet: a band worn round the arm as an ornament.
broad: *broad day*=full daylight.
brooch: ornamental pin worn on the clothes.
bruise: coloured place on the skin caused by a blow.
brute: animal; man who behaves like an animal; *brutal*=like an animal, very
    cruel.
but: (sometimes) only.
butler: man-servant in charge of the dining-room.

C

candlestick: support for a candle.
cane: walking-stick.
canvas: strong cloth used for a ship's sails, tents, etc.
captor: one who has caught (captured) another.
catch: *catch his eye*=make him notice one.
challenge: deny the truth of what has been said.
charity-boy: boy who lived at home but was kept by public money.
chatter: *his teeth chattered*=made a noise by hitting against one another.
cheerless: dull, uncomfortable.
chimney-sweep: man who cleans the insides of chimneys.
chin: the part of the face below the mouth.
choke: to prevent from breathing.
clasp: join tightly together.
class: *first-class*=(slang) the best.
claw: bony, sharp-nailed finger.
cling: hold firmly.
cloak: loose outer garment.
close: *the day closed in*=it became dark.
clue: that which leads one to find the answer to a question.
clutch: seize; hold tightly.
coachman: man who drives a carriage.
cocked hat: hat with its edges turned up.
coffin: box in which a dead body is put.
coil: a set of circles of rope (or wire, etc.).
colour: *he coloured*=his face became red.
come: *to come off*=happen.
commons: *House of Commons*—See House.
comparatively: compared with others.
conclusion: end.
confide: tell secrets to a trusted person.
confine: *confined to*=found only in.
confirm: to make certain.
considerable: not a little.
consult: (sometimes) take into consideration; *consult a watch*=look at—

contempt : scorn; adj. *contemptuous.*
contradiction : disagreeing with what others say.
corpse : dead body.
counsel : to take counsel = ask each other's advice.
counter : long table in a shop on which goods are shown.
countryside : the country round a place.
crack : a crack on the head = a blow.
cradle : baby's bed; childhood.
cripple : one who cannot walk properly because of damaged legs.
critical : the critical moment = the time when one thing or the other may happen.
crust : hard outer part, e.g. of bread.
cuff : turned-up fold of a coat or shirt at the end of the arm.
cunning : clever, deceiving.
customer : person buying in a shop or public-house.

D

damn : curse.
dart : to dart away = move away very quickly.
dash : to dash his brains out = break his head to pieces.
daybreak : dawn, the first light of day.
deadly : deadly fear = very great fear; *deadly pale* = like one who is very ill.
decided : a decided miser = very much a miser.
defamation : damaging the fame or good name of a person.
den : (1) hole in which an animal lives; (2) hiding-place, usually for thieves.
deny : to deny somebody something = not give.
deprive : take away from.
desert : (v.) to leave unprotected; *the street was deserted* = there was nobody in—
destination : place to which one is going; to which a letter is being sent.
directly : immediately.
dismal : unhappy.
dismount : to get down from (a horse, carriage, etc.).
distribute : give out among several people, or in different places.
distrust : not to trust.
dock : place in a court of law where a prisoner stands.
dodger : one who can *dodge* (= escape by tricks) cleverly.
doze : to sleep lightly.
drowsy : sleepy.
duly : as agreed upon.
dwelling : house.

E

easy : easy chair = a comfortable arm-chair.
elbow : (v.) push (as in getting through a crowd).
elderly : rather old.
element : earth was not her element = she was not made to live on earth.
emerge : to come out.
endanger : to put into danger.
envelop : to hide by covering all round.
errand : journey made to carry a message.

exaggeration: adding to the true facts.
exclamation: something said in surprise.
exhausted: too tired to do anything more.
exposure: being out in (the cold, etc.).

F

fair: beautiful.
fatal: ending in death.
fatigue: great tiredness.
feeble: weak.
fell (**p.t.** *felled*): cause to fall.
fist: the closed hand.
fit: a fit of crying = sudden violent crying.
flee (**p.t.** *fled*): to escape, run away.
flight: a flight of steps = a set of stairs.
fly: to advance or fly = go forward or run away.
forcible: by force.
foremost: the one in front.
formidable: causing fear.
fortnight: two weeks.
fraud: deception, dishonesty.
frequent: (v.) go often to (a place).
frightfully: in a frightening way.
frown: to draw down the eyebrows (as when angry).
fulfil: to give what is wanted.
fury: great anger; (adj.) *furious*.

G

gain: to gain the corner = arrive at —; *to gain upon* = come nearer to.
gallows: a wooden framework for killing wrong-doers by hanging them by the neck.
game: the game was up with us = we were caught.
gang: band (of robbers, etc.).
gasp: to take a sharp breath, as when astonished or afraid.
gather: (sometimes) to come to know.
gin: a colourless strong drink.
glare: (n.) very bright light; (v.) to look angrily at.
glide: move silently.
gloom: darkness; (adj.) *gloomy*.
gratitude: gratefulness, thankfulness.
green: (sometimes—slang) simple-minded, inexperienced.
grope: to grope one's way = feel for one's way with outstretched hands.
growl: to make an angry sound like that of an angry dog.
guinea: a gold coin worth £1 1s.

H

half-crown: silver coin worth two shillings and sixpence ($\frac{1}{8}$ of £1).

ham: meat from the leg of a pig, salted.

hand: *to bring up by hand* = feed from a bottle; *take him off my hands* = look after him so that I need not do so.

harsh: rough, unpleasant.

haughty: proud and scornful of others.

haunt: (n.) a place visited often; (v.) (1) to visit often, (2) to keep coming back to the mind.

hay-rick: store of hay (dry grass) built up in the shape of a hut.

headlong: as quickly as possible, without looking to right or left.

heart: *to set one's heart upon* = decide that one must have.

hearty: with a good heart; *a hearty laugh* = loud; *a hearty meal* = eaten with great enjoyment; *a hearty welcome* = full of true feeling.

heel: *to show one's heels* = run away.

hinge: the moving metal part between (e.g.) a door and the door-post on which it turns.

hoarse: rough-sounding, as after shouting too much.

House of Commons: the lower law-making house of Parliament.

housebreaker: thief who breaks into houses.

housemaid: woman servant.

humane: kind and gentle.

humility: n. from humble; *mock-humility* = pretending to be humble.

humour: *in the humour to* = in a favourable state of mind to.

hush: be silent.

Hyde Park: a large open space with grass and trees in London.

I

identify: pick out as the right one; *identity* = who a person is (e.g. you must prove your identity before you can receive money at a bank).

ill-treat: to be cruel to.

impatient: not wanting to wait.

impressive: solemn: *impressively* = in an important way.

impudent: not showing proper respect.

indifference: not caring.

indirectly: as a result, but not a direct result.

inexcusable: that cannot be excused or forgiven.

infallible: which never goes wrong.

infamous: having a very bad character.

inform: *to inform about (against)* = tell the police.

inherit: receive property after the owner's death.

inmates: those who live in a place.

insensible: knowing nothing about what is happening.

inspect: to look at closely; (n.) *inspection.*

intently: with great attention; *intent upon (on)* = attending carefully to.

interest: *to have an eye to one's interest* = look out for ways of making money, etc.

intimate: close (friend).

invaluable: of the greatest possible value.

ironical: adj. from *Irony* (= using words which are opposite to one's feelings— for an example, see Pretty in the Glossary).

J

jailer: prison-keeper.

jerk: (n.) a sudden movement or sudden stop.

Jew: member of a race that once lived in Palestine but now lives in many countries.

jolly: happy, merry.

jug: pot (with handle) for liquids.

jury: twelve men chosen to decide in a law-court whether an accused person is guilty or not guilty.

L

labour: hard labour = a form of punishment in prison.

labourer: farm worker.

lad: boy; *lad of all work* = boy who does work of any kind.

laden: carrying.

lamb: like a lamb = being very well behaved.

lame: having a bad leg and unable to walk properly.

landing: flat place between two sets of stairs.

lantern: lamp that can be carried about.

leaky: having small holes through which water can get in or out.

leave: to take one's leave = to say good-bye and go away.

lecture: speech given to teach (usually many people).

leisure: at leisure = at the time that suits one.

lend: to lend a hand = help.

length: at length = at last.

let: to let = (this house) can be hired.

limp: to walk unevenly because of a damaged foot or leg.

lined: (about a pocket-book—thieves' slang) containing money.

linger: to stay a long time.

lock: a lock of hair = curl of several hairs.

locket: small box made of precious metal, worn round the neck, containing a picture or the hair of a loved one.

loiter: to stand about idly.

loss: at a loss = not knowing what to do.

lots: to cast lots = choose one out of a number of people by a game of chance.

M

ma'am: a form of 'Madam' used by a servant to his mistress.

magistrate: judge in whose court small matters are decided.

majestic: like a great ruler.

maker: her Maker = God.

mark: mark my words = think about what I say.

material: (adj.) real.

mattress: large flat bag filled with cotton or other material used for sleeping on.

maze: many paths turning this way and that way, so that it is difficult to find one's way.

melting-pot : pot used to melt gold and silver articles.

merriment : happiness; laughter.

midst : middle.

might : (n.) power.

mischief : wrong-doing; *to mean mischief* =to have evil plans.

miser : one who saves and loves money too much.

missis : (as used by servants) the mistress.

mist : cloud close to the ground; *a mist came before his eyes* =he could not see clearly because of tears.

mistering : (made-up word) calling someone 'Mr.'.

moan : (n.) low sound of grief or pain; (v.) to make such sounds.

monster : person too wicked to be human.

motion : (v.) to make a sign.

mount : to climb up on.

mournful : sad.

mutter : to speak in a low voice without moving the lips.

N

narrate : to tell a story.

narrowly : she eyed him narrowly =watched him to see what he was going to do.

native : his native place =the place in which he was born.

naval : of the *Navy* (a country's warships).

neck : to bring one's neck in danger =risk being hanged.

new : the New World =N. and S. America; *a newcomer* =one who has just arrived.

nightcap : cap worn in bed.

nightfall : the end of the day.

noose : a running noose =circle of rope which becomes tight when one end is pulled.

nostrils : the two openings of the nose.

O

oath : (1) a promise in the name of God; (2) an evil word.

obscure : little known.

observe : (sometimes) to say.

obstinate : unwilling to obey; not giving up an opinion.

obvious : clear, easily seen.

occupy : occupied =busy.

occur : it occurred to him that =the thought came to him that.

onion : strong-smelling vegetable used in cooking.

oppose : be against; take the other side; (n.) *opposition*.

orphan : child whose parents are dead.

outskirts : the outer edge of a town.

overdo : to do something too much (e.g. act too much).

overhear : to hear words not meant for oneself.

overpower : to conquer by greater power.

overtake : catch up with.

overthrow : upset, cause to fall over.

P

pace: *at a good pace*=quickly; *paces in advance*=several yards ahead.

palm: the flat inside of the hand.

parish: district served by a church; local government of such a district.

parliamentary: adj. from *Parliament* (a body of persons chosen to make the country's laws).

parrot: a bird which can repeat words.

partial: in part.

party: *party to a murder*=one who is responsible in some way for—; *two parties to a bargain*=two people who have made an agreement.

passionate: showing very strong feelings.

patient: (n.) person who is ill.

pauper: poor person, esp. one helped with public money.

pavement: stone footway.

pedlar: one who sells from door to door.

peel: *orange-peel*=the skin of an orange.

peep: (n. & v.) look for a moment.

penetrate: go into; find the answer to.

pepper: hot-tasting powder made from a seed and used with food.

perfume: sweet-smelling liquid.

person: *found on his person*=hidden in his clothing.

pickpocket: one who secretly steals things from people's pockets.

piercing: very cold (air).

pistol: very short gun fired with one hand.

pitch: black.

piteous: showing pity.

pitiful: needing pity; (sometimes) having pity.

plant: (v.) (sometimes) to put.

plunder: (v.) to steal by force; (n.) the act of—

pore: small opening in the body from which sweat comes when the body is hot.

powder: *with a powdered head*=with hair made white by powder (very old-fashioned in Dickens's time).

precaution: care taken before an event.

pretty: *pretty well*=quite well; *pretty treatment*=fine treatment (but meaning 'unfair').

protectress: woman who protects.

prudence: wisdom; not acting foolishly.

pulse: the heart-beat.

pursue: (1) run after; (2) go on speaking; *to pursue one's way*=go on; *pursuers*=those who run after someone; *pursuit*=running after.

Q

question: *out of the question*=not to be thought of.

R

rarity: n. from Rare.

rascal: bad man or boy.

rattle: make a noise as of shaking stones in a tin.
rear: (v.) to look after a child; (n.) *to bring up the rear*=come last.
reduce: to make weak; *to reduce to poverty*=make poor.
reflect: (sometimes) to think; *reflections*=thoughts; thoughts spoken aloud.
regard: to look at.
rejoin: to go back to.
relax: to become less hard.
remainder: what remains.
remorse: deep sorrow for wrong done.
repent: to feel sorry for having done wrong; (n.) *repentance.*
resemblance: looking like (from v. *resemble*).
reserve: (n.) keeping back part of the truth.
restless: wanting to do something but not sure what to do.
restore: to put back as it was; bring back to health.
resume: begin again; continue after a pause.
retire: to move away.
return: — *returned Sikes*=Sikes answered.
revive: to bring back to one's senses.
roll: (n.) small round loaf of bread for one person.
rouse: to wake up; to excite.
ruffian: a rough, lawless fellow.
rustle: to make a noise like moving paper.

S

scaffold: raised wooden floor on which evil-doers stood before being hanged.
scrap: small piece.
Secretary of State for Home Affairs: Minister of the Interior, head of the government office dealing with matters inside the country.
sense: to collect his senses=begin thinking again.
sentence: the judge's sentence=his punishment of a wrong-doer; *sentence of death*= punishment by hanging.
serve: serve him right=it will be a just punishment; *to serve his turn*=help him.
shabby: (garment) old and much worn; (person) poorly dressed.
sharp: at five sharp=at five o'clock exactly.
shawl: loose cloth worn over the shoulders.
shed: (n.) hut; (v.) *to shed blood*=kill.
she-devil: female devil.
shiver: to tremble.
shot: within shot=able to be seen and shot.
shrink: to draw back.
shrug: to draw up (one's shoulders) meaning 'I don't care'.
shutter: movable wooden covering for a window.
single-handed: alone, without help.
skinny: very thin.
slap: to hit with the open hand.
sleeve: that part of a coat, shirt etc., which covers the arm.
slight: (of body) not heavy.
snare: (n.) trap for animals or birds; (v.) to catch in a trap.
snatch: to seize suddenly and without asking.
sneer: smile showing disrespect.
sneeze: to make a sudden outburst of breath through nose and mouth.

snuff: tobacco powder drawn up the nose.
so: so-so = neither good nor bad.
sofa: cushioned seat for two or more people.
soil: (v.) to make dirty.
solitary: lonely; *solitude* = loneliness.
soon: this was no sooner done than = as soon as this was done.
soul: not a soul = nobody at all.
spare: to spare him (from such deeds) = keep, or save, him; *spare my life* = do not
    kill me.
sparkling: flashing light.
spectacle-case: case (box) for a pair of spectacles (eye-glasses).
spectator: one who looks on.
spider: eight-legged creature which makes a web (net) of fine threads.
spill: to spill someone's blood = kill.
splash: to throw out water or mud.
sport: in sport = as a joke.
spot: (sometimes) place.
spring-gun: trap which fires a gun if an animal moves a string.
stagger: to walk unsteadily.
stamp: (v.) to put the foot down noisily.
standstill: brought to a standstill = stopped.
start: (sometimes) to jump with fear.
startle: to surprise and frighten.
steal: to steal a look = look without being seen to do so; *to steal away* = move
    away unseen.
stealthily: secretly, like a thief.
stir: to move.
stop: to stop dead = stop suddenly and not move.
Strand: a street in London.
strangle: to kill by holding the throat tightly.
study: (n.) room for reading and writing.
stumble: to make a wrong step and fall forwards.
suppress: to put down; keep down.
surgeon: doctor who cuts the body to heal it; *surgeon's friend* = something which
    will cause people to need a surgeon.
swamp: soft, very wet land.
swear: to swear somebody = make him swear that he will tell the truth.
swell: (adj.) (slang) fashionable.

T

tear: tore along = went very quickly.
terms: conditions of an agreement.
terrified: full of terror (great fear).
timid: fearful.
tinker: man who repairs things made of metal.
tiptoe: on tiptoe = on the points (ends) of the toes, silently.
toast: pieces of bread made hard and brown on the surface by being held in
    front of a fire.
torch: piece of wood with oil on the end, burnt to give light.
torture: (n.) great pain; (v.) to cause such pain.
train: a train of ideas = one idea coming after another.

136

trap-door: covered opening in a floor or roof.
tremendous: very great.
trial: (sometimes) trouble or difficulty.
trifle: (n.) unimportant thing.
twinkling: in a twinkling = very quickly.

U

undertaker: one who arranges for dead people to be buried.
uneasy: not feeling comfortable; anxious; (adv.) *uneasily.*
uninhabited: having nobody living in it.
upbringing: bringing up, training.

V

verdict: opinion given by the *jury* (see Jury).
vice-president: one who acts for the president. (There is no Vice-President of the House of Commons.)
villager: one who lives in a village.
villain: wrong-doer.
virtues: good qualities.
visible: which can be seen; *invisible* = which cannot be seen.
voluntary: acting of one's own free will, not forced.

W

wag: (v.) to move (as a dog moves its tail in pleasure).
washerwoman: woman whose work is to wash clothes.
waste: to waste away = gradually become thinner and weaker.
web: see Spider.
wharf: place built at the edge of the water at which ships can load and unload.
will: (n.) signed paper in which a person says what is to be done with his property when he dies.
window-blind: cloth pulled down from a roller to cover a window.
wink: to shut one eye without moving the other.
withered: dried up; thin.
womanhood: the condition or time of being a woman.
workhouse: a place for homeless poor people.
workmanship: of fine workmanship = very finely made.
worship: your worship = words used when speaking to a judge.
worthwhile: a good, or necessary, thing to do.
wretch: (1) bad person; (2) sad, poor person; *wretched* = very unhappy.

THE BRIDGE SERIES
General Editor J A Bright